SPE~~CANCELLED~~

This ~~book is published under the a~~

THE ULVERSCROFT FOUNDATION

(registered charity No. 264873 UK)

c/o **The Royal Australian and New Zealand College of Ophthalmologists,
94-98 Chalmers Street, Surry Hills,
N.S.W. 2010, Australia**

OVER HIS DEAD BODY

Ever since Caroline Tucker moved back home from Hollywood to the bright lights of Haven, New Mexico, she's been trying (and failing) to avoid her ex-husband, town sheriff Travis Beaumont. However, she's forced to call him when her niece stumbles across the perfectly preserved body of a cowboy at Girl Scout camp. But is this a crime scene? Or is it just a potential tourist attraction? The mystery of the mummy unravels and Travis digs up some sinister evidence. And the more Caroline tries to keep away from trouble — and Travis — the more they come knocking at her door . . .

Books by Laurie Brown
Published by The House of Ulverscroft:

THE DEATH OF BRIDEZILLA

LAURIE BROWN

OVER HIS DEAD BODY

Complete and Unabridged

ULVERSCROFT
Leicester

First published in Great Britain in 2011 by
Little Black Dress
an imprint of
Headline Publishing Group, London

First Large Print Edition
published 2012
by arrangement with
Headline Publishing Group, London

The moral right of the author has been asserted

British Library CIP Data

Brown, Laurie, *1952 –*
  Over his dead body.
  1. Divorced people- -Fiction.
  2. New Mexico- -Fiction.
  3. Romantic suspense novels.
  4. Large type books.
  I. Title
  813.6–dc23

  ISBN 978–1–4448–1134–6

Published by
F. A. Thorpe (Publishing)
Anstey, Leicestershire

Set by Words & Graphics Ltd.
Anstey, Leicestershire
Printed and bound in Great Britain by
T. J. International Ltd., Padstow, Cornwall

This book is printed on acid-free paper

To my husband Brit, my real-life hero.

Acknowledgements

Many thanks to Leah Woodburn, your savvy editorial input has made this a better book.

To agent extraordinaire Lucienne Diver, thanks for your positive attitude in spite of my whining.

To Mary Micheff, my BFF and critique partner, I couldn't do it without you.

Thank you to my co-workers at Poplar Creek Public Library, especially Darly Doyle, Sue Haisan, Kathy Kirstein and Pat Hogan, for your understanding and encouragement.

Last but never least, thanks to my family for believing in me, for giving me the luxury of uninterrupted time, and for putting up with the roller-coaster life of a writer.

1

When you find yourself somewhere totally unexpected, doing something you never imagined that you'd do in a million years, odds are family is responsible. Only your relatives take you at your word when you say, *If there's anything I can do, just give me a call.* They call.

And since Caroline Tucker had made the mistake of telling her sister she wanted to make up for the last ten years of being away, saying no hadn't been an option. That was why on a warm Saturday in September she was sitting on a rock out in the desert foothills of the Sierra Blanca Mountains of New Mexico, miles away from civilization. She shifted position, trying in vain to find a comfortable spot, yet thankful she wasn't required to lie on the rough ground like two of the other patients.

'You have a broken arm, two broken legs and a serious head wound.'

Caroline tried to hide a smile and failed. Her niece was serious, intelligent and mature for a nine-year-old, but the solemn pronouncement was mitigated by her sweet little-girl voice and faintest trace of a lisp.

'You're in terrible pain,' Julie reminded her with a deadpan expression.

Caroline groaned, acting the wounded patient for five little girls who had eagerly set splints on her limbs and were wrapping them with roll after roll of three-inch-wide gauze and yards of adhesive tape in the single-minded pursuit of the highly coveted First Aid Badge. 'Oops. Not over my eyes, please.'

The mini-medic who was bandaging Caroline's head adjusted the last loop with a mumbled apology. She finished taping the turban just as a shrill whistle marked the end of the test period. All activity stopped and everyone turned to face the central area.

'Good job, girls.' Troop Leader Trudy Ferris applauded, calling out each patrol's bird name-sake as she slowly turned in a circle.

All the girls joined in the applause. Caroline used her free hand to pat her bandaged arm.

'I'll be around to check each patrol in turn,' Trudy continued. 'Once you've passed inspection, you may start on the next badge activity, cooking dinner over a campfire. Remember the plans you made at the meeting. Clear a flat spot and make a circle of stones before you gather wood. We already have plenty of kindling available by breaking up these tumbleweeds, so you're going to be looking for small mesquite branches, some larger ones, and a log or two. Remember, dry wood only. Lay out your fire in one of the patterns we learned, but do not, I repeat do not light your fire until it's checked or you won't get credit for that step. Okay. Buddy system, and don't go farther than fifty yards from this spot.'

One little girl raised her hand. 'How far is fifty yards?'

'Stay within sight of the RV,' Trudy said, pointing to her trailer-sized vehicle that Caroline and one other driver had followed to this remote spot.

Caroline was out of her element acting as a surrogate parent, but unfortunately her sister, Dee Ann, was having a difficult pregnancy. The doctor had put her on bed rest for the next three weeks until her due date. Normally Dee Ann would turn to their other sister, Mary Lynne, for help. The two of them had grown close after Caroline had gone off to California. But now that she'd returned to Haven after her wedding planning business failed, Caroline wanted to reconnect with her family.

Plus Dee Ann didn't have a lot of choice. Mary Lynne was on a cruise with her husband, daughter Belle, and Dee Ann's younger daughter Crystal. So Caroline stepped up and agreed to help her niece Julie with her scouting badges. If she'd known what the job entailed, she might not have been so accommodating.

Did Dee Ann know that this so-called leader allowed the girls to wander off? That she let them play with fire? The sudden protectiveness surprised Caroline, and she had to bite her lip to keep from speaking out. The girls were not appropriate recipients of her opinions.

Their patrol was the last to stand inspection by the troop leader. 'Good job, Hummingbirds. You pass with flying colours, and can start gathering stones and wood.'

'Before they take off willy-nilly, may I have a word with you?' Caroline asked Trudy.

Two of the five girls had already joined hands and skipped off. Julie and the other two stood still and stared at each other with confused expressions.

'Just a moment,' Trudy said before turning to the girls. 'I see we have a dilemma here. Easily solved if the three of you will be buddies.' When the girls did not immediately jump at the suggestion, she said to Julie, 'But what a wonderful opportunity for your aunt to be your buddy. If that's all right with her, of course.'

4

Caroline could tell from her niece's big eyes that she wanted her to say no, but she started unwrapping her arm anyway. 'That sounds like fun.' Not. But at least her niece wouldn't be out wandering in the desert on her own.

The other two girls left in a spate of giggles and the leader took advantage of the opportunity to escape and went to sit in the shade of the RV.

'Wow, this is a lot of gauze,' Caroline said.

With a roll of her eyes, Julie knelt to help remove the bandages. When the other teams returned with booty and left again, she let out a big sigh. 'This is taking for ever. We'll never catch up.'

As soon as she'd freed her arm and Julie had finished unwrapping one leg, Caroline stood to rub her bruised derriere. She tried to flex her cramped muscles and stumbled forward a few steps.

'Can we go now?' Julie asked.

'Ah, did you happen to notice I can't bend my right knee?'

Julie plopped down on the rock.

'It won't take that long to — '

'If I don't help with the fire circle and wood-gathering I won't get the badge.'

The little girl's bottom lip quivered. Either she was a manipulative genius, or failing to

5

get the badge really was equivalent to the end of the world. Caroline just couldn't contribute to that happening. She tested walking with a few stiff-legged paces.

'Okay, I think I can keep up, if you don't run.'

Julie jumped up with a smile bright enough to toast marshmallows. 'Let's go in this direction,' she said before leading off into the sparse desert plants, three- to seven-foot-tall mesquite bushes and assorted cactus. 'No one else went this way,' she added over her shoulder.

After gimping along for twenty or thirty yards, Caroline regretted her decision. The weird gait strained her muscles and the splints had chafed several spots raw. 'Hey, slow down.' She plucked at the gauze wrapped around her leg even as she hobbled along. 'Don't get too far ahead of me. Julie?'

She caught up with her niece in a small clearing. The girl was tugging on the remnants of a good-sized tree that had apparently been unearthed and washed up there with a bunch of other debris by a long-ago flash flood. 'Wow, that's really big. Maybe too big.'

'Can you help me, please?'

'Even if we get it out of that tangle, we'd have to drag it a long way back to camp,' Caroline said.

'We can do it. It's going to be the best log anyone ever found. Pleeeze.'

'Okay. Let's pull together on the count of three.' She took a good handhold on a couple of sturdy branches and counted. With the last number she yanked the tree with all her might. It moved about six inches.

'See. It's working,' said Julie.

Caroline blew out a deep breath. 'Well . . . If I'm going to do any more of this, I need to get this splint off my leg.' She located a rock and crossed the clearing to sit and unwrap gauze.

'Too slow,' Julie said as she followed. She pulled her bum bag around to the front, unzipped it and removed a Swiss army knife.

Fire, and now a knife? What kind of parents were her sister and brother-in-law? Sure, Julie was supposed to be uber-smart, but was that any reason to give her a dangerous weapon?

Julie handed over the multi-tool, opened to the world's smallest pair of scissors.

'I thought your leader said to save the gauze for the next practice session.'

Julie shrugged. 'We probably won't have any more practices, since we all earned our badges today, but if we do, I'll replace this stuff out of my allowance.'

Caroline nodded and started cutting the gauze, soon unsure whether using the tiny scissors was any faster than the unwrapping had been. The exertion was bringing her out in quite a sweat. 'Where is that breeze I felt just now when I need it?'

'Over by the tree stump.'

'Breezes don't work that way. It can't be there and not here just a few feet away.'

Julie gave her one of those looks from under her eyebrows that plainly said her aunt was not as smart as she thought she was. 'See for yourself,' she said with a negligent flip of her wrist. She might just as well have said, *I dare you.*

Caroline Tucker had never turned her back on a dare.

With her head held at a regal angle, she stood and marched towards the log, her stiff leg spoiling some of the effect. Standing arms spread near the upended roots, she waited. Nothing. Hah! She turned to bask in her superiority, and stumbled a couple of steps in her haste. As she recovered her balance, she felt a breeze on the side of her face.

Two steps back, no air movement. Two steps forward, steady breeze. 'Strange,' she muttered. She repeated the experiment several times, until Julie appeared at her side.

'Now do you believe me?'

'It wasn't that I . . . Okay, I didn't believe you. You have to admit, it sounded weird.'

Julie shrugged.

'Grab that branch and let's move this tree out of the way.' Caroline folded the knife and stuck it in her pocket. 'I'll bet this debris hides a cave opening.'

Julie shook her head even as she pulled. 'How did you get from breeze to cave?'

'Change in temperature is the most common reason for air movement,' Caroline explained as they inched the tree stump along. 'Most likely this is a cave connected to others further up in the foothills via a system of shafts and tunnels. Warm air rises.'

'Why?'

'You'll have to ask your science teacher that. All I know is that it's why hot air balloons go up. In this case, warm air going somewhere is creating a breeze.'

'Into a cave?'

'Seems the most likely reason, considering the number of caves in this area.' Then she had another idea. 'Or it could be an old mine. There would have to be another opening farther up the mountainside for the air to circulate, but that's possible. Plenty of old mines have been found all over southern New Mexico. Some treasure hunters believe there is a fortune hidden in these hills.'

'We learned about Chato's gold and Vanderveer's fortune at school when we were studying local myths and legends. Mrs Greenly says they're just colourful stories.'

Caroline squeezed between the branches and a very large rock and came to a sudden halt. A face stared back at her. A scream rose in her throat, and only the awareness of her niece nearby allowed her to stifle it. Though horrified, she couldn't look away from the face. Well, sort of a face. More like a skeleton's head. No, a mummy's. Attached to a dried-up body dressed in cowboy clothes and seated against the wall of a cave entrance.

She spun around and spread her hands in a hopeless attempt to block her niece's view. 'Julie, honey, would you go back to the campsite and ask Ms Ferris to come here?'

A long, high-pitched scream was her answer.

'Or you could just scream like that and she should come running.'

She took her niece by the shoulders. When the girl stopped to catch her breath, Caroline demanded, 'Look at me.' She stared straight into her eyes and said, 'There's nothing here that will hurt you. I promise you.'

Julie swallowed deeply and nodded.

'Good. Now do you want to go sit on that rock while I call Travis?'

The girl shook her head. 'I want to stay with you.'

'Okay. That's fine.' Caroline put an arm around her niece's shoulder as she dialled. 'Hello, Phyllis? Is Travis ... er ... Sheriff Beaumont available?'

'He's out of the office. What's wrong? Are the girls all right?'

Caroline didn't question how Phyllis knew she was on an outing with the Girl Scouts. Aside from being on the force for over thirty years, the woman's network of friends and relatives kept her informed of just about everything that went on around town.

'They're all fine,' Caroline reassured her. 'Will Sheriff — '

'Why don't you call his cell? He's out with Chief Red Hawk of the Tribal Police tracking some drug — '

'I don't have his cell number.' Why would Phyllis think she did? Just because Caroline had been romantically linked to the man once upon a long, long time ago, that didn't mean there was anything between them now. When she'd moved back to her home town of Haven, New Mexico, Travis was just another one of the problems she had to deal with on an ongoing basis. Oh, she was always polite when unable to avoid running into him, which happened way too often, but it was a small town after all. And if her pulse speeded up just a tad whenever he was close, that was of no significance whatsoever and no one knew about it. Not even Phyllis. 'And I don't have a pencil or paper,' she added when the deputy started reciting the number.

Caroline shook her head when Julie offered both. 'Just let the sheriff know we found a mummy, and I would appreciate — '

'I'm sorry. It sounded like you said you found a mummy.'

'That's all I can think of to call him; well, other than Poor Fred, which is what I've named him. Just this second.'

'You mean you found a body in a Halloween costume, like someone wrapped in gauze?' Phyllis said.

'No. That would be me.'

'Huh?'

'Never mind.' She turned, awkwardly due to the half-intact splint, her niece sticking to her side like she was attached with Velcro, and looked at their find. 'I think Poor Fred is what's called a natural mummy. Technically I guess you'd call him a dried-up corpse, but — '

'Can you describe him?'

'His skin looks like brown leather. Eyes are sunken and closed, possibly missing.' Julie groaned, and Caroline patted her shoulder with a muttered apology. 'But he still has a good amount of dirty hair, could be white, or

12

grey, or maybe even light blond. Hard to say.'

'Clothes? Distinguishing marks?'

'He's dressed in jeans and a plaid shirt like a cowboy or prospector would wear. There's a lot of Indian stuff, too, beaded belt, jewellery, and several drawstring pouches. Next to him are two bulging saddlebags and at least one Indian parfleche bag.'

'A what?'

'Parfleche. A rigid box-like storage container with an envelope closure, usually made of stiff rawhide and decorated with mineral paints.' Caroline was proud that she could use the correct term for the item, thanks to the research she'd done for a series of articles on Indian life she'd written recently. Fortunately she'd written a few magazine articles back when she'd been the wedding planner to the stars, and those contacts had led to other magazines and other articles. Although writing didn't pay anywhere near what she was used to making, it kept her busy and just shy of destitute. Oh, for those days of shopping on Rodeo Drive . . .

'Anything else?'

Phyllis's question jolted Caroline back to the present. 'Uh, yeah. There's a ten-gallon hat with the brim stuck under one saddlebag that looks like something straight out of an old Gene Autry movie.'

13

'Any evidence of foul play?'

'Nothing obvious. He looks rather peaceful.'

'Well, don't touch anything. Travis will want to see everything just like you found it.'

Caroline had no intention of getting any closer. 'You don't have to worry about that. How long do you think it will take for him to get here?'

'That depends on your location.'

'The Petersen ranch.'

'Well that cuts it down to a few thousand acres.'

She looked around for some sort of landmark. 'I'm not sure exactly where . . .'

'Never mind. Give me your cell's provider name, and with that and your number I can pinpoint your location via the internet. I'll call you back with an ETA after I talk to the sheriff.'

Trudy, the mothers, and the rest of the girls had arrived. Caroline used her free hand to plug one ear.

'Are you sure the girls are all okay?' Phyllis asked. 'I hear screaming.'

'That's just pre-adolescent female communication.' Something Caroline must have understood at one time but had totally forgotten. Her re-indoctrination lessons had already covered the *a yucky bug just landed*

14

on *the car window right next to my head* scream and the sympathetic group-response scream. And then there'd been the *omigod I was just thinking about the Jonas Brothers and they came on the radio* scream. She still wasn't sure if the dramatic response was because of the coincidence, or for the music, or if it was elicited simply by saying the name of the singing group. Using the scream scale, the mummy was almost as popular as the band.

'I'll call you back,' Phyllis promised before she hung up.

Trudy approached Caroline. 'May I have a word with you?' She motioned for her to step away from the others.

'Certainly.' Caroline flipped her phone closed and gave Julie a little push to encourage her to join the other girls. 'I was just talking to Deputy O'Connor. She'll call back with an ETA after she talks to Sheriff Beaumont.'

'That is a problem,' Trudy said in a serious tone.

'Oh, she probably talks to him every day.' Caroline smiled her best lighten-up-the-situation grin.

Trudy pulled herself to her full height, flipped her long braid over her shoulder and squared her broad shoulders. 'An impertinent

15

attempt at humour doesn't change the issue. You should have waited to talk to me before calling the police. Not only are we on my grandfather's land, I am the troop leader and therefore in charge.'

Although taken aback, Caroline, former wedding planner to the rich, famous and self-important, was not intimidated easily. But she was hampered by the fact that the other woman was probably right. Why had she been in such a tearing hurry to call Travis? Now he would be arriving soon. Perhaps it would be better if Trudy handled everything. 'Sorry. I'm not used to this chain-of-command thing.'

'Apology accepted.' Apparently mollified, Trudy directed everyone back to the campsite. 'I think it's best we continue according to plan until the sheriff arrives.' Then she removed her cell from a pocket in her badge-covered vest and in an aside to Caroline said, 'I don't know what Grandfather is going to say about this. He's a very private man and not too fond of the police. Oh, not Sheriff Beaumont in particular; he just doesn't trust government types in general.' With a sigh, she added, 'Here goes nothing,' as she started towards the other side of the clearing for some quiet and privacy.

Caroline turned for a last look at the

mummy before heading back to the campsite. For a moment she was too stunned to speak. Julie sat on the ground next to Poor Fred while her friend Savannah Remalard took her picture with her fancy phone. Someone had moved the mummy's hand and some of his stuff to make room for the girl to sit.

'Julie!'

She jumped up. 'Ah . . . '

'Perfect timing,' Savannah said. 'Now, Ms Tucker, if you'll just step over here, I can get a few pictures of the person responsible for this momentous discovery.'

'No, I — '

'For posterity. And my website. I blogged about finding the mummy and the numbers I'm generating are awesome. The video hits are already in the triple digits.'

'What?' Blogging, numbers, video hits? Who was this grown-up in a child's body? 'How do you — '

'My dad's in the internet marketing biz,' Savannah explained. 'I was practically born doing stuff on the web.'

'Savannah is going to be a big-time Hollywood director,' Julie added.

'Independent,' she corrected.

'Naturally,' Julie said to her friend before turning back to her aunt. 'And I'm going to star in her movies.'

Just what she wanted for her niece. Not. Oh, Caroline could tell stories about movie stars. Weddings, like any traumatic, life-changing event, tended to bring out the best and the worst in people. The best of Hollywood was usually saved for the cameras. And the worst was the stuff of nightmares. 'Well, don't leave for the coast just yet. Your leader said everyone should go back to the campsite. And we shouldn't move or touch anything until the sheriff gets here to examine the scene.'

Julie's eyes opened wide. 'But I — '

'Do you think it's a crime scene?' Savannah asked eagerly. 'That would be too cool. I'll tape the whole investigation. We'll call it *CSI: New Mexico*. I just love all that whole crime-scene stuff.'

'How about you make a video called *Earning the Outdoor Cooking Badge*? Because unless you hurry, you'll miss the fire-starting.'

With sinus-clearing shrieks, the girls took off running.

Caroline decided she wasn't going to walk another step before getting rid of the leg splint. She found a place to sit, took the Swiss army knife out of her pocket, and selected the scissors. The tiny blades made for slow work, and each layer of gauze had to be cut separately. Despite being well into September, the day was quite warm, over eighty degrees, maybe pushing ninety. She paused long enough to remove her shirt, leaving only her tank top as protection against the fierce sunlight.

Even though the pile of remnants grew, the splint didn't seem any looser. How many rolls of gauze had that girl used? Just as Caroline was considering the wisdom of moving to a place with some shade, a shadow drifted over her and a shiver inched down her spine. She looked up, expecting one of the mothers, or maybe even an irate Trudy to have come searching for her, since she hadn't returned to the campsite as directed.

Squinting into the afternoon sun, she couldn't see much more than an outline. The cowboy hat, broad shoulders, and long legs didn't match the profile of any of the women, and she recognized the ground-eating stride of Sheriff Beaumont. She should have known from the familiar shiver that Travis would soon appear. Every since junior high she'd been able to tell if he was near. Still could, although she'd used her talent to avoid him as much as possible for the last three months. What should she say to him? Just as important, what would he say to her?

'Bad hair day?'

Caroline blinked at the unexpectedness of his comment and unconsciously her hand flew to her head. Dang! She ripped off the forgotten gauze turban, wincing as a few hairs went with the tape. 'You got here fast,' she said, fluffing her short auburn curls while trying to make it look like she wasn't.

Travis took a wide-legged stance and crossed his arms. 'Deputy O'Connor said you found a mummy. Is this some sort of a joke?' he asked as he eyed her up and down.

A second man stepped around Travis.

'We were just over that rise,' Chief Miguel Red Hawk said as he approached her. 'Are you all right?'

'I'm fine.' She held up the scissors. 'Or I will be once I finish cutting my way out of first-aid bondage.'

'Let me help.' He knelt by her leg and pulled a knife from the sheath inside his knee-high fringed moccasins. He paused at her sharp intake of breath. 'Don't worry. I haven't taken any scalps with this. At least not recently,' he added with a teasing grin. 'Do you trust me?'

'Shouldn't I?' Although she looked at him, she was all too aware of Travis staring at her.

Miguel shrugged. 'Apache do not trust easily.'

His casual comment seemed to hide real concern. She smiled at him. 'Last weekend was . . . awesome. I'm so honoured to — '

Travis stepped forward. 'I had no idea you two were dating.'

Caroline turned her head to look up at him over the rims of her sunglasses. 'Maybe that's because who I see and what I do is none of your business.' She straightened her spine and faced away from him. 'But just to clear the air, Miguel and I are not dating,' she said.

'At least not yet,' he said with a grin. 'I told you, I don't give up easily.'

She shook her head. 'We're working together on a project for the New Mexico Historical Society,' she explained to Travis without looking at him. 'I'm writing several articles on the Mescelaro Apache's contributions to the state. Last week I had the singular honour of attending a private ceremony held by Miguel's family to celebrate his little sister's coming of age.'

'Not for publication.'

'I'd never betray your family's trust. But I will write about how deep tribal traditions run, how they are an integral part of your daily life, your very soul.'

'Then my mother was right in her assessment of you, in her decision to include you.'

'Thank you.'

Travis pushed the brim of his hat with one finger until it sat on the back of his head. 'If you two are done with the mutual-admiration do-si-do, can we move along to the reason we came here?'

'Be right with you,' Miguel said as he slid the tip of his blade under the gauze on her leg.

A shiver followed the cool flat back of the knife as it traced a line from her ankle to her thigh. The gauze fell away like a morning glory opening to the dawn.

After sheathing his knife, Miguel jumped to his feet and offered his hand. Caroline took it and stood as elegantly as any princess in a ballroom. She thanked her gallant knight and her smile sparkled in her eyes.

Jealousy smacked Travis in the solar plexus and he coughed to cover his surprised gasp. Then he denied feeling anything other than shock. The three had known each other since school, and Miguel had never shown any interest in Caroline. Of course, she'd been Travis's girlfriend for a lot of that time. Not long ago, Miguel had asked if Travis was getting back together with her. Of course, his answer had been no. Hell, no. And he'd meant it. Had his so-called friend taken that as the go-ahead to make a move on Caroline? Should she be warned about Miguel's love-'em-and-leave-'em style? Hah! More likely his friend should be warned about her.

She hadn't exactly stuck around when the going got tough.

Travis shook those thoughts out of his head. If Caroline wanted to play footsie with the Apache Romeo, it wasn't his place to interfere. Good decision, he reaffirmed to himself.

While he'd been lost in his musing, she'd turned and walked to the far edge of the clearing. He had to rush to catch up. Signalling for them to follow, she slipped behind the pile of brush.

Travis felt a breeze on the back of his neck at the same time the dead man came into view, an eerie coincidence. After ten years in law enforcement in the military and on the Chicago police force, he thought he'd seen just about every sort of corpse: floaters, stinkers, headless, in pieces, with parts missing, you name it. But he'd never seen one dried up like a giant golden raisin. The body resembled one of those Egyptian mummies in the museum with the linen wrappings removed. Except this mummy was dressed like a movie star in a 1940s B Western, with guys named Buck, Hoot or Monte.

As if Caroline read his mind, she said, 'I named him Poor Fred.' She tipped her head to the side. 'Sort of sad that he's been out here all alone.' She turned to Travis. 'How many years do you think it would take to . . . do this?'

'I'm no expert on natural mummification, but I think the time necessary depends on temperature and humidity.' He squatted next to Poor Fred and mentally catalogued details starting with an imaginary outer circle and spiralling inward, just as if he were investigating a crime scene. He took pictures with his cell phone of everything. Close-ups of the thick-soled boots, the copper rivets on the denim jeans and the shell buttons on the plaid shirt, which all appeared unusual and might be significant. 'If it were windy and extremely low humidity, I suppose a body could dry out before decomp set in.'

'Obviously, it's possible,' Miguel said. 'If he died in the winter, low temps would reduce insect activity.'

'Freeze-dried? That makes sense.'

'You guys talk like Poor Fred is a . . . a thing,' Caroline said.

'Sorry,' Miguel said. 'Emotional distancing is a professional hazard.'

'Well, he was a real person and I think it's sad he's been out here all alone. Surely someone was looking for him.'

'Good point. I'll check missing persons as soon as I get back to the station, although it would narrow the search if we had a time of death.' Travis shrugged one shoulder. 'At least a year of death. I wonder if he has a wallet?' He reached to shift Poor Fred in order to check his back pocket.

As quick as a rattlesnake, Miguel knelt and grabbed his arm before he got within inches of the mummy. 'Based on many of the objects, this mummy is probably of the People.'

'I can't believe you're playing the NAGPRA card,' Travis said, but he pulled back and held up his hands as if signalling surrender.

'You bet I am,' Miguel said.

'What's NAG . . . whatever you said?' Caroline asked.

'The acronym stands for the Native American Graves Protection and Repatriation Act, which protects human remains, funerary goods, sacred artefacts, and objects of cultural patrimony. If the body of a Native American is discovered, regulations delineate procedures for initiating consultation — '

'That only pertains if the body is found on federal or tribal lands,' Trudy said, stepping around the men and standing next to the mummy. She laid her hand on his head. 'My grandfather owns this property, therefore NAGPRA doesn't apply.'

'You're mistaken. This is reservation land. And that mummy could be Apache. Look at the traditional beadwork design on those pouches. And the painted design on the parfleche might lead to a particular family, because patterns used on household goods are often passed from generation to generation.'

'And that bag over there has a swastika on it,' Trudy pointed out. 'Does that make him a Nazi?'

'Actually, it might,' Caroline said. All eyes turned to her. 'What? I'm just saying Poor Fred might be a Nazi.'

'In the middle of the Tularosa desert?' Travis asked. 'I thought he might be a lost pilot, but I think he'd have run out of gas before getting here from Germany.'

'And there's no plane,' Trudy pointed out.

'No horse or car either,' Miguel said.

Caroline crossed her arms and stuck out her chin. 'During World War II, there was a POW camp near Las Cruces where many of Rommel's Afrikakorps were sent after they surrendered. If one of the prisoners had escaped, he might have wound up here.'

'Are you joking?' Trudy asked. 'Where do you dig up this stuff?'

'The library, 'Caroline said with a shrug. 'I've done research for tons of magazine articles. Trust me, if there's useless trivia involved, you want me on your team. If you ever need to build a yurt, grow heritage tomatoes, or make a pillow from an old sweater, I can help.'

'I didn't know we had POWs in New Mexico,' Travis said. 'I wonder if there are any records of escaped prisoners.'

'Before you go off the deep end and contact Washington or the German Embassy,' Miguel said, standing, 'the swastika was used in various forms by many civilizations, including the Hopi and Navaho. Both tribes discontinued its use after the war, but this brave could have lived prior to that time.'

'Stop referring to him as an Indian,' Trudy said. 'He could be a prospector . . .'

'No mining equipment,' Travis pointed out.

'Or a cowboy.'

'Without a saddle?'

'Maybe he's a fugitive, or a tourist who wandered off, or . . . or even a Nazi, okay?' Trudy threw her hands up in the air. 'I don't care. I need to get back to the girls. Grandfather is sending his foreman to collect everything, and you guys can deal with him, because I'm done.' As she spun away, she flipped one hand for final emphasis, and accidentally smacked Poor Fred.

Caroline reached to keep the mummy from tumbling, then, apparently realizing what she had in her hands, gave a little moan of distress. Travis was already moving in her direction when she looked to him for help. He righted the body and smoothed back its hair, but took the opportunity to surreptitiously examine the head for clues. What he found was not totally unexpected.

'We should get that paperwork started,' Miguel said, stepping back and turning to the side as if making room for Travis to be the first to leave.

'I'll call you as soon as I'm ready to release the body,' Travis said. He moved the hair aside so that the others could see the round bullet-sized hole in the left side of the skull. 'Seems Poor Fred was murdered, and this is now officially my crime scene.'

Miguel crossed his arms, his face suddenly stony. 'Must I point out again that we're on reservation land. This is now my crime scene.'

Travis gave him a hard, unblinking stare.

After a moment's silence Miguel said, 'Perhaps in the interest of diplomacy we should share jurisdiction of the site until the ruling of an agreed-upon cultural expert can be obtained.'

'Okay by me.' Travis flipped open his phone and called for one of his deputies to guard the area. While he listed the equipment he wanted Bobby Lee to bring, he gazed at the thin spiral of smoke from the scouts' campsite. The problem with Caroline, he thought, was that she had a penchant for finding trouble. He looked around the wide-open site and decided two deputies should stand guard while he and Miguel went into town to start the necessary paperwork.

2

'What are all these people doing here?' Travis asked when he returned to the cave area later that day. He waved his arm to encompass the surrounding area, thankful the deputies had cordoned off the crime scene with yellow Do Not Cross tape.

To the left of the cave entrance four elderly Native American women dressed in traditional garb sat in a line and chanted what he assumed were blessings for the dead. In the fading light of early evening a news van from EI Paso pointed its headlights towards the cave and a smiling blonde reporter in ridiculous high heels interviewed several hippies in front of their VW bus. A Japanese tour group in identical shiny black suits and an assortment of wild cowboy hats and hand-tooled boots enthusiastically snapped pictures.

'Since when is a crime scene a tourist attraction?' Travis grumbled. 'These people should be ogling evidence of invaders from outer space at the Alien Museum or getting their pictures taken with the World's Largest Pistachio.'

'Isn't it amazing?' Bobby Lee Tucker said. He was the youngest deputy in the department with all of nine months' experience on the job, and one of Caroline's brothers. 'Most of these people read about the mummy on the internet and came all the way out here just to see it.'

Travis could only shake his head. There was no figuring some people. 'Where's Harlan?' he asked. Harlan Keyes was the other deputy he'd inherited upon agreeing to return to Haven and take over the job of sheriff from his grandmother after her stroke.

Travis hadn't hung around town after Caroline had left him. He'd done a little motorcycle racing before the military, and then he'd joined the Chicago police force. Almost a year ago, he'd taken a leave of absence to help his grandmother during her recovery. Lou Beaumont was certain she would resume the duties of the position she'd held for more than thirty years. Travis wasn't so sure that was a good idea. Even if she were capable, he was concerned that the stress that came with it would bring on a second stroke. When he'd brought up the idea of putting himself forward for the job, she'd been thrilled, even though it meant she'd be forced to retire permanently, because it also meant he wouldn't be returning to Chicago.

31

Even if he hated to admit it, the fact that Caroline had moved back had been a major factor in Travis's decision to stay in Haven. Although he doubted they had a future together, he needed to resolve this tangled, complicated thing between them once and for all, if that was possible.

Travis shook his head and realized he'd not been paying attention to Bobby Lee's answer. 'Sorry, my mind was wandering.'

'Understandable, since this crime scene isn't like any other and presents unique problems.'

Like he was thinking about Poor Fred. 'Where did you say Harlan is?'

'That real nice Girl Scout leader invited us to come to their campfire for dinner.'

'So of course Harlan jumped at the chance.' Deputy Harlan Keyes was the thirty-five-year-old son of Haven's mayor, who'd often stated that his dear boy deserved to be named interim sheriff during Lou's absence. In Travis's opinion, the 'dear boy' needed to grow up first and learn to pay more attention to his job than his stomach.

'To be truthful,' Bobby Lee said, ducking his head, 'I lost the coin flip. Whatever they're cooking sure smells good.'

Travis had been trying to ignore the delicious aroma, because he hadn't taken time to eat since breakfast. 'Maybe you can snag yourself a plate while you fetch Harlan.'

Bobby Lee was gone before the last word was spoken.

Travis reset his hat more firmly on his head and headed towards the visitors, even though he dreaded the inevitable confrontation with Arlene Couch, the alpha-female pit bull of news reporters.

'Sheriff Beaumont?'

Travis stopped in his tracks and spun around at the sound of children's voices. One little girl held out a plate of food and the other an icy glass of lemonade and several biscuits on a napkin. Caroline stood behind them with a folding chair in one hand and a salesgirl's smile pasted on her face.

'We thought you might like something to eat,' Julie said.

'Actually, we didn't even know you'd returned,' Caroline said. 'We were bringing dinner to Bobby Lee, but he passed us on his way to find Harlan. He suggested we bring this to you.'

Travis went down on one knee in front of the girls. 'Smells wonderful. Did you cook this yourselves?'

'We made the biscuits,' Savannah said.

'And helped chop the vegetables,' Julie added.

'I appreciate your thoughtfulness,' Travis said, taking the plate and piling the biscuits on top before accepting the lemonade. 'Would you young ladies care to join me for some dinner conversation while I enjoy this magnificent repast?'

Both girls eagerly nodded yes even as Caroline declined. 'We really should be getting back. Isn't that right, girls? You don't want to miss the campfire sing-along.' Then she remembered the chair she'd brought and unfolded it. 'There you go,' she said.

After placing a hand on each girl's shoulder, she steered them around and pushed them back towards the campsite.

'I thought you always hated camping,' Travis said in a low voice.

She hesitated a moment. 'Go ahead, girls, I'll be right behind you,' she called after them before turning to face him. 'I'm here for Julie.'

'Commendable,' he said, sitting in the chair. It even had a cup-holder for his lemonade. 'Are you staying the night?' he asked before taking a large bite of food.

A casual question flipped her way in the same manner one might ask about the weather, or last night's TV programme. Yet the familiar husky timbre of his voice made the enquiry seem suggestive and intimate.

'In a tent with five nine-year-old girls and a teenage scout working on her mentor badge. You?'

'Are you asking if I'm going to stand guard over the crime scene all night?'

'Isn't that what deputies are for?' a deep voice said from behind her.

She turned to see Police Chief Miguel Red Hawk approaching with a handsome man dressed in khakis.

'I hope I'm interrupting a private conversation,' Miguel said with an unrepentant grin. 'No? Too bad.' He introduced Dr Aaron Dichali, Cultural Anthropologist and Archaeology professor at the University of New Mexico Las Cruces, and the consultant chosen to determine if the mummy was a Native American. He explained that Caroline was the one who had discovered the mummy.

Travis stood up and placed the plate on his chair before shaking the man's hand. 'Thank you for coming so quickly.'

'No problem,' Aaron said. 'I was over at Three Rivers Petroglyphs Park scouting this semester's archaeological site.' He turned to Caroline. 'We start digging next week and always welcome locals if you're interested.'

She shook her head.

'Let's discuss it over lunch tomorrow,' he urged. 'Maybe I can pique your interest.'

Caroline laughed at his sophisticated but barely disguised come-on line. 'Sorry, but I have a business appointment.'

'The mummy is this way,' Travis said, as he unsmilingly directed the newcomer across the clearing with a wide sweeping motion.

The handsome professor held out his arm to Caroline. 'Would you accompany me? You can tell me all about how you came upon such an extraordinary find.'

She glanced over her shoulder in the direction the girls had taken. 'I guess I won't be missed for a few minutes.' She took his arm and they walked away, leaving a shocked Travis and Miguel.

'You shoot him and I'll scalp him,' Miguel said under his breath.

'Make that offer again after we get the evaluation, and I just may take you up on it.'

3

Caroline waited until the second to last of her charges entered her house and the mom waved; then she backed her car out of the drive and headed for her sister's house.

'Can I talk to you?' Julie asked in a small voice.

'Sure.' She glanced over at her niece to see her biting her lip. 'You can tell me anything.'

'I think I've done something really bad.'

Caroline pulled over to the kerb and shifted the car into park so she could give Julie her undivided attention. She twisted sideways in her seat. 'Why do you think that, sweetie?'

Julie dug into her backpack and pulled out a small carving of an eagle's head on a two-inch-thick circular base. 'I took this, and now I'm cursed.' She stroked the head with one finger. 'It's so beautiful and it seemed like the mummy wanted me to have it.'

Caroline blinked. 'You are not cursed.' She might be in violation of that NAGPRA thing Miguel had talked about, and therefore open to arrest and a thousand-dollar fine but other than that . . . 'Tell me what happened.'

'Well, Savannah wanted a live person in the

picture for the human interest angle. So I sat down next to Poor Fred, and I guess I must've bumped him or something because his arm moved and this rolled right into my lap. Like he was giving it to me.'

Caroline held out her hand, and even though Julie hesitated, she gave the eagle statue to her aunt. The piece would be called rustic in style, but the carver had paid meticulous attention to detail. Each feather had been scored, and the bird's haughty stare gave it a regal air.

'Am I going to jail?' Julie asked, tears in her eyes.

'Of course not,' Caroline said, and forced a laugh as she leaned over to give the girl a hug. That was the truth. No way was she going to let that happen. 'Tell you what. After my appointment, I'll stop by the site and simply put this back in Poor Fred's hand. No one will ever know.' And if they did, she would take the blame.

Julie sighed, but Caroline couldn't tell if it was in relief, resignation or grief at losing the tiny figurine.

After confirming the girl had nothing else she wanted to talk about, Caroline dropped her off and went home to shower and change before her appointment. She chose to wear her best skirt suit, the pastel-pink vintage

Chanel giving her confidence a sorely needed boost.

She'd never planned a reaffirmation of vows ceremony before, but according to Trudy, her grandfather wanted it to be as much like a wedding as possible. They'd gotten married at the county courthouse soon after WWII ended, without any sort of party or reception. Trudy quoted Mr Petersen as saying, 'This will be the wedding we never had.'

So far, Caroline had only spoken to Trudy's grandmother. Enid Petersen had described her vision of the event as a big party with family and friends at which sometime in the evening she and her husband would surprise their guests by standing up and renewing their vows.

Either way, Caroline couldn't afford to turn down business or to not work on a Sunday afternoon if that was when the client wanted to see her. Not if she wanted to keep up with the rent on her shop. Last week she'd booked a themed birthday party for a seven-year-old and nineteen of her very best friends who were all going to be princess brides.

Caroline pulled up the gravel driveway neatly lined with rounded river rocks and turned into a parking area large enough to hold six or eight cars. She made a mental note to discuss guest parking arrangements as she gathered her sample book and laptop.

Most people in the area called their country properties ranches, but the Petersens always referred to their place as a farm, and now she could see why. The white clapboard farmhouse with green shutters looked a bit out of place among the brown adobe outbuildings and multi-hued gardens, rather like a large pale woman surrounded by tanned children in colourful garb.

When a woman in her forties answered the door, Caroline introduced herself.

'Ms Enid is expecting you. Please follow me to the atrium.' While she led the way at a quick pace, the woman continued, 'My name is Bev Frye. I've been keeping house for the Petersens for sixteen years and I hope to continue for another sixteen. Ms Enid is an angel, purely and simply an angel.' Bev opened a set of double doors leading into a large greenhouse where colourful exotic plants spilled from shelves stuffed with all manner of pots and containers. 'No finer a woman is walking this earth today, except maybe my mother, and sure as the forecast for tonight is dark, that'd be right difficult to call one way or t'other.'

A tinkle of self-conscious laughter met them at the door. Enid Petersen stood about five feet tall. Her grey hair was arranged in a neat bun, and she wore a simple cotton dress with a pattern of small pink roses. She stepped forward as she removed a bright green gardening glove and stretched out her hand. 'So glad you could come, Caroline. Oh, I guess I should ask if you *are* Caroline.'

Again that same bell-like laughter. She sounded so much like Glinda the Good Witch from the classic *Wizard of Oz* movie, Caroline half expected to spot the Yellow Brick Road and Munchkins hiding among the flowers.

'But then who else would you be?' With a smile, Enid motioned her deeper into the room, shutting the doors behind them. 'I have to keep out the cold air,' she explained. 'My husband, Jurgen, is a great believer in arctic-level air-conditioning, but my plants disagree.'

Caroline didn't admit it out loud, but she was definitely in the arctic camp. Not only was the conservatory a bit warm for her taste, the lining of her suit jacket was already sticking to her arms.

'Bev will bring us some tea,' Enid said. 'That is, if you'd like some iced tea?'

'Sounds perfect.'

The room wasn't overly wide but it was quite long. Their heels clicked on the tiled floor as they walked to the far end, where two chairs flanked a bistro table stacked high with gardening magazines that Enid quickly moved to a nearby shelf.

'My apologies. I'd intended to straighten up in here earlier but I got distracted by my aphelandra blooming.' She motioned to a plant with zebra-striped leaves and an eight-inch spike of a golden flower. 'Not a rare occurrence in the botanic world, but my first.'

'Your plants are amazing,' Caroline said. Some of them were large enough to merit first names. Like the four-foot-tall plant covered with yellow flowers that she would name Yolanda. This woman had a serious green thumb. 'Absolutely amazing.'

Enid shrugged as if was nothing. 'Growing things is in my genes. My father was a farmer, and his father and back for generations. In fact, my family was among the first settlers in this area.'

Caroline had a brainwave. 'Why don't we use your plants as table centrepieces?. We could put them in matching containers . . . ' She paused when the older woman grimaced. 'Or we could wrap the pots in matching foil paper and ribbon.'

Enid smiled. 'That would be nice and colourful and wouldn't disturb the plants unnecessarily.'

'Have you decided on a particular colour scheme?'

'Blue is my favourite. But I also like yellow because it's so cheerful.'

'We can do mostly blue with touches of yellow. That would be lovely.' Caroline, writing in her notebook as she talked, was startled by a booming voice calling for Enid. The older woman covered her mouth, not quite stifling a nervous giggle. 'You must excuse my husband's manners. He's used to working with farmhands,' she said in a whisper as she stood.

'Enid! What are you doing? I thought we were going to meet with the wedding planner in the living room.'

Caroline noticed that Mr Petersen had a slight German accent.

'We're coming, dear,' Enid said, scooting sideways in a crablike shuffle as she kept her attention on Caroline and hastened her forward with frantic hand movements. 'I was just showing Caroline the aphelandra,' she called over her shoulder.

They exited the atrium, and Enid introduced her husband. Jurgen Petersen had a military presence with his close-cropped white hair, rigid posture and uniform-like pressed khaki pants and shirt. His handshake was firm and brief.

'I'm sure you understand that I'm a busy man so you won't mind getting right down to business,' Jurgen said as soon as they were seated, him in a leather wing-back chair and the two women on a chintz-covered sofa. He picked up a folder from the table and laid it on his knees.

Caroline sat on the edge of the cushion to keep from sinking into the overstuffed softness. She opened her notebook on her lap. 'Enid and I were just talking about — '

'Yes, yes, that's all well and good. Now please take notes, as I don't like to repeat myself. We will invite two hundred guests.'

'Oh, Jurgen, that's too many. We don't have that many friends and — ' Enid's husband cut her off with a glare so brief Caroline wasn't sure she'd really seen the venom in the look.

'We have customers and suppliers who will expect to be invited. I have prepared a list.' He handed over a sheaf of pages. 'The invitations should be mailed by Friday, so I will expect you to deliver a proof by Tuesday.'

'Wait a minute,' Caroline said. 'We haven't even set a date.'

'I told Enid to inform you that we wish to do this on our anniversary in three weeks.'

'She did,' Caroline lied, not sure why she

felt so protective of the older woman. 'But three weeks is not enough time to plan a wedding.'

'If we keep it simple,' Enid whispered, 'maybe — '

'We will have the proper wedding that circumstances denied us,' Jurgen insisted, not letting his wife finish her sentence. 'Are you saying you cannot do it?' he asked Caroline, his arched eyebrows all but daring her to admit defeat.

'Not at all. But if it's to be done so quickly, certain accommodations must be made. First I'll see what venues are available. There aren't many places in town that will accommodate two hundred guests. Are you willing to relocate the event to El Paso?'

'We will have it here,' Jurgen pronounced. 'At the house.'

'Oh, yes,' Enid said, her cheeks flushed. 'As a girl I dreamed of getting married outside beneath an arbour of flowers and then dancing the night away under the stars to the music of Artie Shaw, Duke Ellington, Dizzy Gillespie and especially Glen Miller. 'String of Pearls' is my all-time favourite song.'

'I noticed a grassy meadow behind the house that appears ideal, nice and flat.'

'The horse pasture?' Jurgen asked with a horrified look.

'With some work it could be lovely,' Enid said.

'We could bring in tents and a portable dance floor,' Caroline said, jotting notes as she talked.

'A tent? You want to hold a wedding in a tent? We are not Bedouins. What's wrong with having it indoors like normal people?'

'Really just a tent roof,' Caroline explained to Jurgen. 'The sides will be open for air circulation. The advantage of holding the event outdoors is that we'll be able to accommodate the number of guests you want.' She glanced significantly around the living room. 'I mean, this room is large and all, but even if everyone stood the entire time you could only pack sixty to sixty-five people in here. Where are you going to serve food? Are your guests going to eat standing up? And you can forget dancing.'

'Fine!' Jurgen threw up his hands. 'We'll get married in a tent in the horse pasture. But I will concede on those two items only. Everything else must be traditional. Exactly as a wedding would have been in 1946.' He stood and set his shoulders. 'Enid knows my wishes. I shall leave the rest of these tedious details to you women.' He gave a curt nod and left the room.

Caroline blinked. She wasn't quite sure

what to say to that.

'Please excuse Jurgen. He sometimes finds it difficult to express himself even after all these years of speaking English. He came to America as a prisoner of war, you know. We met when my father hired POWs to work in the fields.'

'No, I didn't know that.'

Enid retrieved a photo from the bookshelf. She traced the figures with one finger for just a moment before handing the picture to Caroline.

The pudgy girl in the sepia photograph had a crown of blonde braids and a shy smile. She was dressed in a simple shirtwaister of some light material sprigged with tiny flowers. The young man wore a suit, probably borrowed, because it was too long in the arms and legs. If not for the fact that it was also too tight across the chest, he would have looked like a boy who was supposed to grow into the suit over the next two or three years.

'You look so young and sweet,' Caroline said.

Enid tipped her head to the side as she looked at the picture too. 'Naïve,' she said. 'I was fifteen years old, and the few farm boys I'd known were nothing like this sophisticated foreigner. From the moment I laid eyes on him, I was determined to marry him. My father was quite upset about my infatuation, as he called it. But I persisted, and Jurgen and I found stolen moments to speak. He was taking English lessons at the POW camp and I think that at first he responded to my chatter simply to practise his vocabulary.'

'It's a romantic story.'

Enid ducked her head and shrugged. 'The prisoners were released in March and we planned to get married the following spring. That fall, my father was killed in a hunting accident. Jurgen and I went to the courthouse and got married right away so he could move in and help me with the farm. Life wasn't easy with just the two of us to do all the work.'

Caroline nodded sympathetically to encourage her to continue. Sometimes the most important part of being a wedding planner was being a good listener.

'When I got pregnant, he recruited another former prisoner who'd decided to stay in the area. Walther was a bit strange. Wouldn't come in the house, not even to eat. I couldn't decide if he was more scared of me or terrified of being closed in again, but whatever his reasoning, I rarely caught a glimpse of him. I left his meals on a table on the back porch and the following morning all the dishes from the previous day would be returned clean and neatly stacked. Jurgen said he slept outside in a blanket roll most nights, just inside the barn door if the weather was bad.'

'Sounds like a reaction to his imprisonment.'

Enid nodded and sighed. 'He would sometimes leave me small thank-your gifts, mostly pretty rocks and cactus plants that he found on his desert wanderings; once a change purse he must have traded the Indians for. Such a gentle soul, a sad case. I've kept Walther in my prayers ever since the day he decided to take off.'

'Where'd he go?'

Enid shrugged. 'I don't know. Jurgen said he'd always wanted to see the Pacific Ocean and that he'd probably headed for California.'

'But you never heard from him?'

'No. I don't even know if he could read and write. I'm glad Jurgen didn't react the way his friend did. Although I suspect his incarceration might be one reason why he's so ambitious. To this day he's always on the lookout for more efficient methods, better seeds, more land.'

Whenever the conversation paused, Caroline asked questions so she would understand what the bride wanted. They were nearing the end of her standard questionnaire on items such as favourite colours and favourite flowers when she suddenly put her hands to her head.

'Is something wrong?' Enid asked, her brow furrowed with concern.

'I just had a brilliant idea, like a bolt out of the blue.' Caroline waved her hands around in her enthusiasm. 'Jurgen said he wanted your reaffirmation of vows to be exactly as a wedding would have been in 1946, didn't he?'

'Yes,' she said, hesitation obvious in her tone.

'Let's do exactly that. A themed reception. The wedding party will dress in the fashions of the forties. Even the guests will be encouraged to get in the spirit. We'll choose music from that era.' Caroline clapped her hands. 'We could book a live swing band. Wouldn't that be fabulous?'

Enid's eyes sparkled, but she held her tongue.

'The wedding you always dreamed about,' Caroline said. 'Say you'll do it.'

'Jurgen also said he wanted traditional.'

'We'll do everything that was traditional in 1946.'

'I still have . . . Do you think my mother's wedding dress would be appropriate?'

'What could be more traditional?'

Enid smiled. 'Let's do it.'

'Fabulous.' Caroline leaned forward and gave the older woman a hug. 'Now, I have so much to do.' She jumped up and gathered her things. 'I'd better get started on the research immediately.' She turned to Enid. 'I'll email you a basic proposal tomorrow. Menu possibilities and stuff like that.'

Enid shook her head. 'I don't have an email address yet,' she explained as they walked to the door. 'I know, I know. My children tell me I'm a dinosaur because I don't network.'

'My mother refused to get a computer until a few years ago. Now she's better at that social networking stuff than I am.'

'I'm trying to get caught up with this century so I can stay in touch with my grandchildren: I've signed up for a class at the library,' Enid added in a whisper.

'We're in such a time crunch, I can't wait for snail mail. I'll stop by tomorrow with a proposal.'

They set the time for ten o'clock and Enid showed her to the door herself.

As Caroline walked to her car, she mentally measured the horse pasture. Room there to have separate tents for dining and dancing. She shook off a shiver of foreboding, but the strange feeling followed her all the way to the car and persisted as she took off her jacket and hung it on a hook over the back seat window. It was still there as she drove down the driveway, despite all the ideas for a forties-themed wedding swirling around her brain.

Her car had always functioned as a refuge, an island of relative silence, because she never talked on her cell while driving. Oh, she'd had any number of earphones and headsets, but after using each new attachment a few times she'd relegated all that stuff to the trunk. Even in LA traffic, even when her business had been at its most hectic, driving had given her time to think, to prioritize.

Haven wasn't exactly the fast lane, but she still had plenty of worries. There was Mimi, her grandmother, who had as much as admitted she was dying and then refused to discuss the matter any further. There was her fledgling event-planning business and her article-writing, which at least was paying some bills. Dee Ann was going to need some extra help when the new baby arrived. There had been her cousin Barbara's murder, but Travis had helped clear Caroline's name and had arrested the guilty party, so at least that issue was closed. But it had forced her to face the fact that she still felt . . . something for her ex-husband. She wasn't sure what it was or what it meant to her future, only that the feelings could neither be denied nor ignored much longer.

She purposefully switched mental gears and focused on the errand she needed to perform for her niece. At the crossroads she swung her car to the right and headed west towards the Sierra Blanca Mountains. Already the setting sun had painted the foothills in purple shadows and streaked the sky with the palest of pinks and springtime yellows. After a few more turns she started looking for the turn-off that was little more than a few tracks in the dirt.

If there'd been any question as to which dirt road to take to the campsite, an enterprising entrepreneur had solved that problem. On the side of an ice cream truck a hand-lettered sign proclaimed *This Way to the Mummy* above a large arrow. Below that it said *Sno-Cones $1.00*. Caroline didn't stop, but returned the vendor's friendly wave, wondering how he could possibly have enough business to make his trip out into the desert worthwhile.

She soon found out she needn't have worried. As she approached the former campsite, Harlan waved two flashlights at her like he was directing a 747, guiding her into the temporary parking lot cordoned off with orange caution tape. She counted thirty-one cars, four tourist buses and half a dozen vans as she searched for a parking spot. With so many people around, she wouldn't have a chance to put the little eagle statue back into Poor Fred's hand. She tried to come up with Plan B while she parked.

Why hadn't she thought to bring a change of shoes? The nude pumps with four-inch heels showed off her legs to advantage and made her look taller and more in charge, but they weren't appropriate for walking in the desert. The temperature outside was way too warm for her to put her suit coat back on. Her lace camisole and pencil skirt would have to suffice. She straightened her shoulders and grabbed her purse.

As Caroline entered the clearing, she blinked at the changes less than twenty-four hours had brought. The brush had been totally cleared away and a generator ran power to several strips of powerful lights. To the left of the cave a dozen Native American women sat in a semicircle and chanted while three younger women shuffled back and forth in a solemn dance. To the right a refreshment stand had been hauled in and was doing a brisk business selling tacos, burritos and quesadillas. A couple passed her on the way to the parking lot each carrying a plate of *tres leches* cake that looked homemade, and so tempting that she almost decided to give up her quest and get in the long line at the snack bar.

She half expected to find her younger brother performing his deputy duties somewhere near the food truck. Considering Bobby Lee's prodigious appetite, it would be perfect. Thinking of him inspired the idea of giving him the statue to return. She dismissed that thought almost as soon as it occurred to her. Not fair to put him in the position of choosing between family and his job.

'Aunt Caroline?'

She spun around. 'Julie? What are you doing here?'

'I came out with Savannah and her dad.' She pointed towards the cave. 'They're taking more video because her website has had so many hits.' She looked around before lowering her voice and asking, 'Did you put it back yet? Of course not. You can't with all these people watching. I'm so cursed.'

Caroline leaned over to whisper in her ear. 'You're not cursed, so stop saying that. I've got it in my purse and I'll figure out a way to put it back.' She sensed someone watching her and looked up. Even from across the clearing she'd felt Travis's stare. Getting close to him was about as welcome as cosying up to a thorny cactus, but at the same time he just might be the solution to her problem. She patted Julie on the shoulder. 'You run along and stay with Savannah. I have to see a man about an eagle.'

Julie followed her aunt's line of sight then turned back with a sly grin. 'I get it.' She gave a thumbs-up before scurrying away.

Caroline straightened her back and smoothed her pencil skirt over her hips before approaching him. 'Hello, Travis.'

'No.'

'I beg your pardon?'

'Whatever it is you want me to do, that you know I won't want to do but that you're going to ask me to do anyway because you think you can talk me into it, the answer is no.'

'You got all that from *Hello, Travis*?'

He raised one eyebrow. 'Your eyes sparkle with the challenge and you're sticking your chin out just a tad with determination.' He shrugged one shoulder and gave her a cocky grin. 'You underestimate my memory if you think I can't tell when you're trying to seduce me.'

'Hold it right there, cowboy.' Caroline backed up a step and held up her hands between them. 'You're throwing a saddle on the wrong horse. No way am I seducing you.'

'You want me to do something I don't want to do. That's a second cousin with the same name to convincing me to do something I already want to do.'

Was he saying he *wanted* her to seduce him? And why had the ambient temperature suddenly shot up twenty degrees? 'You're reading way too much into a simple greeting.'

'Am I?' He crossed his arms and tipped his head down to give her a steady stare.

Was that the stance he used when interrogating criminals? If so, she totally understood why he had the reputation of breaking even the toughest suspect. She felt the need to confess . . . everything. 'I ran a stop sign on the way here. And I confess I ate the last three chocolate chip cookies even though I let Mimi think Bobby Lee did it.' She bit her lip to stop herself babbling.

After a moment's silence Travis said, 'Far be it from me to stop you before you get to the interesting stuff, but maybe you should just ask me whatever you got all dressed up and came all this way to ask.'

'I had a business appointment.'

'No need to get defensive.' He smiled. 'When I said if there's anything I can do, just ask, I meant it.'

Sure he did, but only because he never expected her to ask. Well, she didn't have a lot of choices if she was going to keep Julie out of trouble. She took a deep breath as she glanced around to make sure no one was within earshot, and saw Miguel and that professor from the University of New Mexico heading their way. What rotten timing, but at least she'd seen them beforehand so she wasn't in the middle of blurting out her question just as they walked up.

After the usual handshakes and greetings, Travis apologized to Caroline for the interruption and promised to call her later. He then suggested they move to the cordoned-off area of the cave so they could discuss the mummy away from the crowd. In other circumstances Caroline would have appreciated the brush-off as an opportunity to get away from Travis. But she wasn't willing to give up on her mission just yet, so when the professor turned and waved to her in an unspoken invitation to come with the group, she followed eagerly. If she could get close enough, she could either drop the eagle into the cordoned-off area or pitch it into the nearby bushes if she had to.

'I didn't expect to see you again so soon,' he said.

'Nor I you, Dr Dichali.'

'Aaron,' he insisted. 'I decided to give Sheriff Beaumont and Tribal Police Chief Red Hawk the results in person because I'm interested in what will happen next.'

Caroline looked up at him in surprise. 'You've finished your evaluation so quickly? I expected it to take longer. Don't you have to wait for test results or something?'

'No intrusive tests are allowed, so I only have my observations. After checking a few references, this case seems quite simple.'

'Okay, Doc,' Travis said, turning to face Aaron as the group reached the perimeter of the cave.

Caroline noticed the slight widening of his eyes when he spotted her and she flashed him a wide smile.

'What's on your mind?' Travis asked Aaron, ignoring Caroline.

'I've finished my evaluation. I declare that Poor Fred,' Aaron nodded toward Caroline to acknowledge the use of her name for the mummy, 'is a European male from the beginning of the twentieth century.'

'And you came to that conclusion how?' Miguel asked, his face a mask of stone.

'I estimate him to have been five foot eight or nine, a bit above average for the time period. The measurements of his facial features are similar to those of middle European people. The clothes appear to have been new at the time of his death. You'll notice there's no wear observable on the elbows of the shirt, or the knees of the jeans.

Since the clothes are typical Western wear of the late forties, I conclude he was an unfortunate traveller new to the area, not a resident or a Native American.'

Travis immediately dialled his cell phone. 'Okay, Phil, it's officially our crime scene. Get the coroner out here. Did you find any legal reason for me to chase off the lookie-lous? Well, keep at it.' He hung up and shook Aaron's hand. 'Thanks, Doc. You'll understand that I now have lots to do, so please excuse me.'

'Hold on a second, Kimosabe,' Miguel said. 'I protest. What about the beaded pouches and the painted parfleche? Have you tried to trace the decorative patterns to a tribal or family origin? How did you take measurements without touching him?'

'The beaded artefacts are quite common, the type used in trade and made for sale to tourists. Admittedly the measurements were extrapolations from photographs, but that's an acceptable procedure, admissible in court.'

Miguel turned to Travis.

'Don't look at me,' Travis said. 'You chose the expert.'

'Well, I'm un-choosing him and filing a protest.'

'Judge Macky will be in his chambers

tomorrow morning at nine o'clock sharp,' said Travis.

'The mummy is on reservation land,' Miguel reminded him.

'Not according to my GPS, but you can add that to your dispute.'

Miguel crossed his arms. 'You're not going to wait until I can get a — '

'Nope,' Travis answered. He stepped around his friend to see if the mummy had any ID in his pockets.

'Nothing there. Let's see what's in the parfleche, for starters. This one's heavy.'

'I feel like a kid on Christmas morning,' Aaron whispered to Caroline.

Travis opened the flap and tipped the bag so that the contents slid out.

'Damn.'

4

When Travis tipped out the contents of the parfleche, there was a collective whoosh of indrawn breath at the sight of dozens of baseball-sized rocks tumbling on to the woven blanket. Clear white-faceted stones laced with wide streaks of gold. As bright and shiny as when they'd been packed away.

'Wow. That was unexpected,' Aaron said, blinking.

'That stash of gold must be worth thousands of dollars,' Miguel said. 'Are those diamonds?'

'Probably white quartz. Not very valuable, but commonly found around and among gold deposits,' Caroline said. 'I researched gem-stones and minerals found locally for an article in *Rockhound* magazine.'

'I'm no expert in mineralogy, but that looks like a lot of gold to me,' Aaron said. 'Hey, maybe this guy is the fabled Vanderveer and that's his fortune.'

Two more parfleches and one of the saddlebags revealed more gold. Travis care-fully counted and took pictures of the rocks before packing them into evidence bags. The other saddlebag had a set of new clothes similar to the ones the mummy wore, with the sales tags from Joske's Department Store still on them.

'I never heard of them,' Caroline said.

'Not surprising. You were probably in kindergarten when they were bought out,' Aaron said. 'I got my first grown-up suit there,' he added with a laugh. 'Man, I hate it when something reminds me I'm getting old.'

'My mother says the same thing.'

'Ouch, that hurt.'

'Sorry. Maybe I should introduce the two of you.'

Aaron placed his hand over his heart. 'Must you mortally wound me? Do you really think I'm old enough to date your mother?'

'You're too used to young co-eds seeing you as another Indiana Jones.'

When Aaron grinned at the comparison, Caroline rolled her eyes and turned away. 'Why would someone kill Poor Fred and leave him here without taking the gold?' she asked Travis. 'Did they not know about the gold? Does this mean he was a prospector or a miner, even though he doesn't have any tools?'

'All good questions,' Travis said. 'Hopefully when we solve the crime, we'll have good answers.'

At least he hoped they'd have the answers.

The coroner arrived, driving the Rondale Funeral Home hearse right up to the cave entrance with horn blasting and a flashing red light on the roof, scattering people every which way.

'That was quick,' Travis said to Marlene as soon as she hopped out of the vehicle. She was near as tall as him and wore her blonde hair in one long braid down her back. Although they'd grown up in the same town, he'd only known her as the pesky girl her brothers were often forced to bring along. He'd been surprised to find she'd been elected county coroner and pleased to learn she was quite good at it. 'Where'd you get the cherry?'

'Isn't it cool? I wanted a bar like the one on your patrol cars, but it was too hard to take off and put back on. This light attaches with magnets, runs on four D-cell batteries and is operated by a remote control.' She kept up a spiel of chatter as she opened the back cargo door, pulled out the gurney, and unpacked her stuff. 'I picked it up at this booth with all kinds of neat retro stuff at the last Law Enforcement Trade Show. You gotta go with me next time.'

'How did you get here so fast?' Travis asked, ignoring the invitation. Since he'd been back in town, she'd hinted that she'd be willing to give a relationship a try, but he just couldn't get past the memory of the little girl who'd made her brothers and their friends attend the funerals of her dolls in the back yard.

'I started out as soon as I saw Dr Dichali arrive. Didn't even wait for Joey to get back from his supper break.'

'Wait a minute. You said you *saw* him?'

'I was monitoring the situation on the streaming video feed. When I saw the gold, I figured I'd better beat feet to stay ahead of the crowd, so I turned on the lights. I'll hurry this along because things are going to get ugly fast. Do you think I should get a siren?'

'No.' After a momentary pause, Travis asked, 'What do you mean, ahead of the crowd?'

Marlene didn't pause in her work of manhandling the gurney over the stony ground and into the cave entrance, leaving Travis to trail after her. With a movement of her head she signalled for him to look back over his shoulder at two girls, one with camera in hand, standing just beyond the chanting Native American women.

'Those are the Girl Scouts who brought me dinner last night,' he said.

'Then you've met the geniuses behind

Desert-mummy's-little-helpers.com. Once their video showing you finding gold goes viral, you're going to have treasure hunters flocking here like vultures around a ripe carcass.'

Before he'd taken three steps in the girls' direction, Marlene called his name and he turned back.

'It may not be any of my business, but after I take the body, what are you going to do with the rest of the stuff?'

'Do you have anyplace to keep the gold for a few hours until I can get someone to open the bank vault?'

'Not gonna happen. The only vault in town is on a timer.'

'I could lock it up in a jail cell, but right now everyone on duty is out here working crowd control. I don't want to leave it unattended, but if I don't move it, these people will never leave.'

'I can put it in my cooler until you get this place cleared.'

'Does it lock?

'Not really. But it's guarded by three corpses inside and my poodle Georgie on the outside.'

Marlene's dog might be a miniature, but he had enough meanness for a full-sized mastiff. Travis suspected the little dog was always angry because Marlene dressed him in frilly outfits. The last time he'd encountered the malicious furball, he'd suggested Marlene buy him some leather and chains.

'That's good enough for me. Take everything and I'll get back to you in the morning.'

'You got it.'

'Bag and tag.'

'I know. I know.'

Leaving Marlene to do her job, he spun on his heel and stomped towards the girls. But Caroline anticipated his move and arrived before him to stand in front of them with her arms spread protectively. He pressed his lips together to keep from smiling. Did she really think she could stop him if he was determined to get by? And why was she protecting them? It hurt to think she believed him subhuman enough to harm children.

'I'm not going to hurt them,' he said, his voice gruffer than he intended.

'I never thought you would,' Caroline said without moving out of his way. 'But that ferocious scowl on your face will scare the bejeesus out of them. They're only little girls.'

'Those *little girls* — '

'Calm down. Now why do you want to talk to them?'

'According to Marlene Rondale, who is knowledgeable about that sort of thing, the video those two little girls have posted online is going to go viral. Then every crackpot treasure hunter from here to Timbuktu will descend upon Haven. And that, my dear, will make it near impossible for me to investigate this murder case without tripping over — '

'That's no reason to scare — '

'I just want to ask them to voluntarily take down their site for a few days. And they don't look scared to me.'

Caroline turned around. The two girls were holding hands and singing, 'Our video's going viral, our video's going viral,' while dancing in a circle.

'I don't think they're going to be interested in taking down their website,' Caroline said over her shoulder to Travis. She shook her head at their antics, even though she was smiling. 'Seems strange to me that videos shot by and narrated by children would be of any interest to anyone except their relatives. I'll talk to them later, after the excitement wears off.'

The girls stopped jumping up and down and Savannah pulled her cell out of her pocket. 'Hi, Daddy. Are you ready to go home? What? OMG. Yes, yes, we'll meet you at the snack bar in fifteen minutes.' She hung up and stood there blinking.

'What's wrong?' Julie asked.

Savannah grabbed her friend's arms. 'We

just rolled past fifty thousand hits and we're on three most-watched lists.' The girls squealed and jumped up and down like two game show contestants who'd just won a car. Two cars.

Travis wasn't nearly as excited. Nor was he as amused at the situation as Caroline appeared to be. 'Of course you realize that means your face has popped up on over fifty thousand computer screens,' he told her.

Her jaw dropped. Just a little, but he always noticed everything about her. A habit forged in childhood that he hadn't been able to break. He had to turn away to hide a smile he couldn't hold back and didn't want to explain.

Across the clearing, Marlene was talking to an aggressive-looking man with white-blond hair. She pointed in Travis's direction, obviously trying to get rid of the stranger so she could complete her task. 'Excuse me,' he said over his shoulder to Caroline as he headed in that direction to break up the quickly escalating confrontation before all hell broke loose.

Not that he feared for Marlene's safety. She had a black belt in karate, bench-pressed near two hundred pounds, and she'd grown up with five brothers. She could take care of herself. It was the stranger he was concerned about. How far would Marlene go if sufficiently annoyed? He was worried she'd forgotten about the streaming video.

As he strode towards the cave, he sized up the pushy stranger. A bit taller than Marlene, so that made him about Travis's height of six foot three. He appeared to be in his forties or possibly early fifties, but he had the lean athleticism of someone who ran or maybe swam marathons. His custom-tailored suit bespoke money and power even with the jacket off and thrown over his left shoulder. From his cleverly casual haircut to the tips of his genuine alligator shoes, the stranger obviously meant to impress. Travis recognized the effort and wondered why.

After Marlene had introduced Karl Arndt Volker, she left the two men and continued her work. Karl offered his business card instead of his hand. Without taking it, Travis quickly read: *Volker Aerospace Technologies*, an address in Potsdam, Brandenburg, Germany, and *President/CEO*.

'You're the man in charge?' Volker asked. His English had only the slightest trace of an accent.

'Aerospace technologies? If you're looking for the White Sands Missile Range or the German Air Force Training Center at Holliman, you're in the wrong place.'

'I have come a very long way because I am sure that mummy is my grandfather.'

'Really? And the gold has nothing to do with it?' Travis was quite aware that a trans-Atlantic flight would have taken more time than had elapsed since the revelation of the treasure had hit the internet. So the question was, had Volker really come all the way from Germany? Easy enough to verify.

'I did not even know about the gold until I got here.'

'The Apache still claim the mummy is a Native American.'

Volker swung his suit coat off his shoulder and removed a packet of papers from the breast pocket. 'Here. I have been researching my grandfather for the last six months.'

'Oh really, huh?'

Volker narrowed his eyes and glared at Travis, who grinned back.

'On her deathbed, my grandmother confessed to living a lie for more than sixty years. Her husband had not died a hero's death while serving in Rommel's Afrikakorps as she had always claimed. She knew he'd been a prisoner of war, because she received monthly letters until March of 1946. Then nothing.'

'Surely there was a record of what happened to him.'

'All the government would say was that

71

they had no record of him after Rommel's surrender. She was so ashamed that he had not returned to her and the baby he'd never even met. She made up the details of his death from stories she'd heard other war widows tell.'

'So you grew up thinking of your grandfather as a big Nazi hero and don't believe — '

'I am named after my grandfather. I admire him for serving his country, for doing his duty. The fact that an evil monster was at the helm of the government was not Grossvater's fault.'

Travis nodded to Volker to continue.

'From the POW records that the United States transferred to the Deutsche Dienststelle Archive in Berlin, I traced my grandfather's unit from Africa to Tunis, across the Atlantic, by train to Fort Gruber, Oklahoma, and Camp Bixby, a branch camp near Tulsa. In July 1944 they were moved to a sub-camp at Fort Bliss near Las Cruces. That is where the majority of his letters originated. That is not far from here, right?'

'Fifty, sixty miles.'

'Two or three days by horse?'

Travis had to agree. 'Las Cruces, huh?' He'd had a chance to do a little research of his own. 'I read somewhere that only the most diehard committed Nazis were transferred there.'

Volker bristled at the implication. 'My research does not disagree, but one brush cannot paint all figures. If a moderate soldier were assigned to a barrack with rabid Nazis, he would have to reflect their attitudes or suffer the consequences. There is at least one account of a group of top Nazis beating a fellow prisoner to death because they believed him to be a communist.'

'Okay, I'll give you that point. Your grandfather might have been a moderate.'

Volker bowed ever so slightly. 'So the question is, how could he have sent letters from a POW camp for nearly three years and yet there be no record of him being there?'

'The letters were forgeries?'

'My grandmother saved them. All on standard POW letters forms, with both American and German censorship stamps, and crossed-out blocks where material was concealed. The handwriting is his. Genuine.'

'How were they signed?'

''Your loving husband', of course.'

'No name?'

'She knew his name.'

'Ah, but did she know the name he was using in the POW camp?'

'Are you saying he became a prisoner

under an alias? Why would he do that?'

Travis shrugged. 'I read that many prisoners lost their papers in the process of being captured, either accidentally or on purpose. Some changed their name, maybe to avoid the stigma of surrendering. Others changed their rank in hopes of better treatment.'

'That is a good point that I hadn't thought of. Still, in March of 1946 the prisoners were transported by train to the coast for their journey back across the Atlantic, and there is no record of Grossvater either arriving in New York or sailing to England with his unit.'

'So? If he were travelling under an alias . . . '

'But he never returned home. I was at a loss as to what could have happened to him until I saw the video on the internet and everything fell into place. He must have escaped the POW camp and perished trying to cross the desert on foot. All I need is a hair sample, and the DNA test will prove my claim.'

'Whoa, cowboy. If we give a hank of hair to every treasure hunter who wants to run his own DNA test, not only would we have a bald mummy, we'd have hundreds of so-called descendants clamouring for their inheritance.'

'Are you insinuating I would falsify a DNA test?'

'Doesn't matter. Until I solve the mystery of what happened to Poor Fred, he's off limits to everyone.'

'Who?'

'Sorry. That's just what we've been calling the mummy, for lack of a better name.'

'His name is Karl Arndt.'

'I get it. You think he's your grandfather. I'll make a note of your claim. But this is not a simple case. There's a lot of gold involved, and the mystery includes more than just his identity. I need to find out who murdered him, and why.'

'Someone murdered Grossvater?' Volker's hand went to his throat and his pale face blanched even whiter.

Travis could only shake his head. Either this guy was on the level, or he was an expert con man.

Marlene called him over. 'With Miguel and Aaron's help I got everything loaded,' she said, and handed him a clipboard with a list of all the materials.

'Thanks, guys.' Travis scrawled his signature across the bottom of the page. 'I couldn't pull the deputies away from crowd control.'

'No problem,' Miguel said.

'I enjoyed it,' Aaron added. 'I only regret that we didn't have time to go through everything with a fine tooth comb.'

'That will be the job of the technicians at the crime lab.'

'Maybe,' Miguel said. 'Only if my protest is turned down. Isn't that right, Sheriff?'

'Sure,' Travis answered, distracted by watching Caroline usher the two little girls to the snack bar, greeting Savannah's father, and then heading towards the parking lot with them.

'The only thing better than watching a beautiful woman walk towards you is watching one walk away,' Aaron said.

'If she looks back over her right shoulder, you should go after her,' Miguel said to Travis. 'If she looks back over her left shoulder, I'll go.'

'And if she doesn't look back at all, I'll go,' Aaron said, hitching up his chinos.

'Yeah, right. You wouldn't get three steps in her direction before someone . . . ' Miguel glanced significantly towards Travis, 'shot out one or both of your knees.'

Travis looked down and realized he was still holding the clipboard. He promptly gave it back to Marlene. 'When you leave, I'll give you a few minutes to get down the road before we start moving this crowd out of here. Sorry for the delay; I'm . . . I lost my train of thought.'

Marlene chuckled as she tossed the clipboard into the rear compartment of the hearse and closed the cargo door. 'Take two aspirin and call me in the morning.' She opened the driver's door, slid into the seat, and turned on her newest toy, the flashing red light.

After checking to make sure she had sufficient room to back up, Travis thumped twice on the roof with the flat of his hand. 'All clear.'

He wished he could say the same about everything else.

★ ★ ★

Caroline walked to the parking lot with the two still-giggling girls and Savannah's father, Rob Remalard.

'I'd be glad to take Julie home,' she offered.

'No, no, no,' Savannah cried. 'She's spending the night at my house. Her mother already said it's okay. We're going to barbecue and put beads in our hair and everything.'

Caroline gave her niece a questioning look, and Julie nodded anxiously.

'Why don't you stop by for burgers and hot dogs,' Rob said.

'No thanks. I still have some to work to do tonight.'

'And don't forget that other thing,' Julie said.

'I won't,' Caroline promised. Not that she knew what she was going to do with the eagle statue now that the mummy and all his stuff had been moved. She just knew she wouldn't forget about it. As she waved goodbye to the girls, she felt Travis gazing in her direction, rather like a magnetic pull that swung her personal compass towards him. She resisted the compulsion.

Caroline returned Marlene's wave as the Rondale Funeral Home hearse, red light flashing, horn blaring, barrelled down the line of parked cars and swerved on to the access road. She had enough sense to jump into her own car and slam the door shut before the blossoming trail of dust following the hearse overtook her.

She encountered little traffic on the way home to her grandmother's house, where she was still living along with her brothers, the newly employed Bobby Lee, and the ex-con Bobby Ray. They were each saving money, hoping to move out sooner rather than later.

The rent on her little storefront business included a second-floor apartment, but she'd hesitated to move in due to Mimi's health. She had learned that her grandmother had a serious condition, but the stubborn woman refused to say more. And the next best source of information, Mimi's best friend Lou

Beaumont, had proved surprisingly mute on the subject. Fortunately Lou lived next door, so Caroline continued to look for opportunities to question her. Unfortunately, Travis lived with his grandmother, making it more difficult for Caroline to avoid him.

She and Travis had a lot of history, very little present, and as far as she could see, absolutely no future. Sure, they'd been childhood sweethearts and had eloped in high school, but their quickie divorce had been the main reason she'd stayed away from Haven for ten years. They'd worked those old hurts out now and she'd forgiven him, but that didn't mean she was ready to get back on the fast train to heartache. Even if her grandmother insisted on matchmaking.

Although it wasn't very late, she was surprised to find Lou and Mimi in the kitchen sharing a pot of herbal tea. Their conversation stopped abruptly as if they had been talking about her.

Mimi jumped up and ushered Caroline to the table. 'You've been so busy, I feel like I haven't seen you all week. Sit. I saved a plate for you. You haven't eaten, have you? No? I knew it.' As Mimi talked, she bustled around the kitchen, taking a covered plate from the refrigerator and popping it into the microwave, setting out napkins and utensils, filling

79

a tall glass with ice and pouring sweet tea into it. 'I'd have iced tea with you, but it's not decaf and these days it keeps me awake. Never used to bother me, but these days I stick with herbal, especially after dinner.' Mimi shook her head.

'Is that because ... you know ... ' Caroline struggled for the right words. She couldn't just blurt out *because you're dying*. Even though it was the main reason she'd decided to move back to Haven.

'Nonsense. I'm just getting old.'

'You've lost some weight,' Caroline pointed out.

'A few pounds,' Mimi admitted with a smile. 'I've been cooking healthier since you've been home.' She took the plate out of the microwave and set it on the table. 'That's wholewheat pasta, and the sauce is made from organic tomatoes.'

'Thank you.'

'And you've been walking every day with me,' Lou added.

'We're up to two miles and it has built up our strength,' Mimi said. She heaved a sigh. 'The mornings are so lovely. Sometimes Travis joins us and we take our coffee to the park. I enjoy listening to the birds. You should join us some morning. Caroline?'

'Huh?'

'Are you all right? You're staring at your plate. Are you trying to read the spaghetti like tea leaves?'

'Sorry. Guess I'm more tired than hungry.'

Mimi stepped over and gave her granddaughter a hug. 'Then go to bed. We'll talk some other time.'

'I'm fine.' She twirled her fork in the pasta. 'I couldn't sleep anyway. I have a ton of things to do for my newest client, a vow renewal ceremony for the Petersens with a nineteen forties theme.'

'Enid Petersen?' Mimi said.

'Do you know her?'

'She was five or six years ahead of us at school. Very shy, very quiet. Doesn't come to town much. She has four daughters, I think.'

'Everyone was shocked when she quit school and eloped with that ex-POW,' Lou said. 'I tell you, she's a saint to have put up with him all these years. A saint.'

'Her name came up recently but I can't remember the context,' Mimi said.

'Isn't one of her granddaughters married to Owen Ferris, the fire chief?' Lou asked.

'Trudy Ferris,' Caroline said. 'She's Julie's scout leader.'

'That must be where I heard her name,' Mimi said, but her tone lacked conviction.

'I like Enid,' Caroline said. 'I really want to

81

give her the wedding she always dreamed of having as her vow renewal, but it's such a short deadline.'

'You'll do a fabulous job,' Mimi said, patting her hand. 'You always do.'

There was a knock on the door and Mimi opened it to Travis. 'I've come to walk Lou home,' he said, remaining just inside the door.

'Are you hungry?' Mimi asked. 'Come on in and have a seat. I'll fix you a plate of spaghetti.'

'No thank you. But as long as I'm here, I'd like to speak to . . . ' Travis looked over Mimi's head, 'Caroline.'

'Sure.' Mimi stepped aside, but neither senior citizen voluntarily left them alone, and their studied nonchalance failed to cover the fact that they were listening avidly.

Travis cocked his head towards the right and Caroline followed him into the hallway just past the kitchen entrance. She didn't want Mimi or Lou to hear, but then neither did she want to be alone with Travis.

'Our earlier conversation was interrupted,' Travis said. He lowered his voice when she placed a finger over her lips. 'I'm not sure if I should be concerned, or if I'm simply curious. What did you want to ask me?'

'I have something to show you, but I can't

do it now, not with them watching. Can you meet me in my office tomorrow afternoon?' No, wait. Her one-girl office was too private. 'Better yet, I'll stop by *your* office.'

'I'm not sure how long the mummy situation will take. Even if Miguel gets his injunction, I've got to find a place to keep Poor Fred and all his stuff.'

'This . . . matter won't take long.' Caroline turned her back to the other women and practically mouthed the words. 'It concerns Poor Fred.'

'What?'

She motioned for him to lean down and whispered the words into his ear. Then she stepped back to get away from his tantalizing scent and seductive warmth, moving so hastily that she backed into the door jamb. 'Ouch.'

'Are you okay?'

'I'm fine.' Why did she always get so clumsy around him?

Travis grinned knowingly at her. Before saying his proper goodbyes and escorting Lou out the door, he told Caroline he'd find a way to meet her the next day.

Mimi had cleaned up the kitchen, as if keeping busy nearby were a valid excuse to eavesdrop. But that was okay with Caroline, because she needed to get going on the

Petersen plans. She picked up her briefcase and laptop case.

'You're not going to start working now, are you?' Mimi followed her down the hall, wiping her hands on a red-checkered dishtowel.

'Short deadline.'

'But even in high school you always did better skipping the all-nighter and getting a good eight hours of sleep. Why don't you go on upstairs and get ready for bed. I'll bring you some graham crackers and a cup of warm milk, just like when you were a little girl.'

Caroline smiled and obeyed. She didn't have the heart to tell Mimi that she had usually dumped the milk and gotten back up to study once her grandmother had gone to sleep.

And then there'd been the times she'd sneaked out to be with Travis.

* * *

When Caroline got out of the shower, she found that Mimi had left a tray on the dresser. She carried her cup of milk to the window seat. From there she could see her neighbour's big garage. Travis had been working on restoring his old motorcycle.

84

He'd said it helped him to organize his thoughts and work out problems. Not tonight, though.

She nibbled on a graham cracker, the kind with cinnamon on top, her favourite since age five, when Travis had shared his lunch with her in kindergarten. Her thoughts kept coming back to him. She had no other choice but to see him tomorrow, give him the eagle, and ask him to help her.

She retrieved the eagle and settled back into the window seat, tucking her feet beneath her white cotton nightgown with eyelet trim around the neckline and on the shoulder straps. She turned the tiny statue over and over in her hand while she tried to think of a story to tell Travis that wouldn't involve Julie, playing the scene in her mind one way and then another.

Suddenly there was a faint click. If the night hadn't been so silent, she might have missed the sound. She looked around, and then down. In the base of the statue a tiny drawer had popped open. A secret drawer that she had no idea how she'd activated. She pulled it open a bit further. There was a folded-up piece of yellowed paper inside.

She should probably wait until tomorrow when she saw Travis to read it, shouldn't she?

The drawer was so small and the paper

packed in so tightly, she couldn't get her finger inside. But tweezers pulled the little half-inch by half-inch bundle out easily. She unfolded it carefully and flattened it smooth on the bed.

She couldn't read the writing, not so much because it was faded, although that didn't help, but because it appeared to be in a foreign language. German was her first guess, but it could be Dutch, of which she knew none.

The rest of the paper was covered with what appeared to be a map. Caroline let out the breath she hadn't been aware she was holding. Was it a treasure map? Was this the location of a gold mine? Did X really mark the spot?

With a pounding heart she gently refolded the map and replaced it in the drawer. With a little trial and error, she figured out that the trigger for the opening mechanism was activated by pushing on the left claw, simple to find once she knew it existed. She put the statue inside a small jewellery box, then put the box and her tweezers in her purse.

If the map actually led to a stash or a gold mine, the tiny statue could be much more valuable than she'd ever dreamed.

There wasn't a snowball's chance in H E double hockey sticks that she was going to get any sleep now. With that thought she dumped the rest of the warm milk down the bathroom sink, sat down at her desk, and powered up her computer.

5

Dressed in her dove-grey silk crêpe business suit, Caroline bounded down the stairs at ten minutes past eight o'clock. Her plan was to leave early and stop by the sheriffs office to hand over the eagle to Travis before going on to her appointment with the Petersens.

She paused at the foot of the stairs and faced Thurston. The large solid brass eagle perched on the newel post had been named after her great-great-great-grandfather, whose portrait in the library sported a similar baldness and fierce expression. She reached up and gave Thurston's head a rub for good luck, as generations of Tuckers had done daily, polishing it shiny smooth and slightly flat.

She set her computer and briefcase on the hall table and went into the kitchen to fill her travel mug with coffee.

'Why did you wait — '

'Wah!' Caroline jerked and slammed her mug on the counter. 'You scared me half to death.'

Her brother Bobby Ray shrugged.

'What are you doing up so early?' she

asked. Bobby Ray was a night owl, always had been. 'By the way, you look like five miles of bad road.'

'Gee, thanks.' He rubbed his unshaved chin. 'I just signed off after a full night.'

'I'm sorry.'

Her brothers might both be named Bobby, after various relatives, but they couldn't have been more different in looks or temperament. Bobby Lee, the sheriff's deputy, was the clean-cut, whistle-in-the-dark, life-of-the-party, everybody-gotta-love-me youngest of five children. Bobby Ray, middle child, ran his internet and radio ministry for ex-cons from home because he was on house confinement for another six months as part of his parole agreement. He rarely shaved, and favoured beat-up jeans and old T-shirts with the sleeves cut out, claiming his clothes were not important because he was never seen by anyone outside the family.

'So why were you waiting to come downstairs until after Bobby Lee left for work?'

'What makes you think — '

'Come on, sis. I'm neither deaf nor blind. I saw the light under your door and heard your keyboard off and on during the night. I do get up to walk around every now and then, for circulation if nothing else.'

'Where's Mimi?'

'In her studio, as you well know. She's the only artist I've ever heard of who works regular hours.'

'She says inspiration is only valuable if you're in a position to take advantage of it.'

Bobby Ray rolled his eyes. 'I've heard all her homilies too. And don't try to change the subject. Why were you waiting to come downstairs?'

'Well, I wasn't waiting for Bobby Lee to leave.' She crossed her heart with two fingers.

'Then what . . . Ah, never mind, I get it.' He gave her a smirk and a wink.

'What's that supposed to mean?'

'Means I understand.'

She turned and nonchalantly filled her cup. He couldn't possibly know she'd hidden up in her room, waiting until she was certain Travis wouldn't be stopping by for coffee as he often did. Sure she wanted to meet with him that morning, but in a public place with other people around, not just a brother who would disappear so they could be alone. 'There's nothing to understand.'

Bobby Ray laughed. 'If you say so.'

Caroline raised her chin and headed for the door, but stopped and turned when Bobby Ray called her name.

'Think fast.' He threw an apple in her direction.

She hadn't completely lost the reflexes that growing up with two brothers had given her, and she reached out and snatched the fruit out of the air. She pumped it triumphantly above her head. 'Thanks for breakfast,' she said, before sticking out her tongue and making a face at him.

Without standing, he executed a respectable bow.

Caroline turned quickly to hid her smile.

★ ★ ★

Travis returned to his office after an early-morning command appearance in Judge Macky's chambers. The judge was in a foul mood after being woken at home by a call from the Governor, who was in a foul mood because he'd received an early-morning complaint call from the president of the Mescalero tribal council. Although Travis had expected an injunction to be issued, Miguel hadn't wasted time or left anything to chance.

When Travis literally ran into Caroline at the door, he automatically wrapped his arm around her waist to keep her from falling backwards.

'Oops, I didn't see you,' she said.

'Sorry, I didn't expect you . . . ' The hold only lasted a few seconds until she regained her balance, but the warmth of the contact lingered.

She laughed, more a nervous giggle. 'As long as we're both here, do you have a few minutes?'

'Sure.' He held the door open and waited for her to re-enter, and then lifted a section of the service counter to allow her to pass through. 'Come into my office,' he added, automatically indicating the way with a gesture.

'Here is fine,' she said, taking a seat at Bobby Lee's desk, her back to Phyllis, who was manning dispatch in the corner of the main room. Caroline took a small box out of her purse, and as soon as Travis sat down, she slid it across the desk. 'That belongs to Poor Fred,' she whispered.

He raised an eyebrow and opened the box. 'How did you gain possession of this?' he asked, examining the small carved eagle.

'I can't tell you.'

Travis stopped and stared at her for a few seconds. He knew that if he pressed she would make a clean break of it. She'd never been able to lie to him. But he didn't need to do that, because he'd already figured out what must have happened. Her niece had taken the bird statue, and when Caroline learned of it she'd insisted it should be put back where it belonged. Unfortunately, that wouldn't be easy now that almost everything had been catalogued.

He was tempted to push it back across the desk and tell her to forget the whole thing. But he couldn't. He held the statue up between two fingers and turned it this way and that. 'What's his name?'

'What makes you think I gave him . . . or her a name?'

He gave her the are-you-joking look from under his eyebrows. 'Because ever since you were a kid you've named everything. I always thought it was cute . . . in a psycho-ward-inmate sort of way,' he added so she wouldn't think he was attracted to such nonsense.

She shook her head and then, looking off to the side, mumbled, 'His name is Ernest.'

Travis smiled and put the little eagle back in the box.

'Wait, there's more,' she said, and held out her hand. After he gave her the statue, she showed him the latch that released the small drawer. She removed the folded paper with her tweezers and handed it to him.

He unfolded the paper and spread it out on the desk. 'Is this what it appears to be?'

'I think so,' she whispered, and with a nod

towards the deputy, placed her finger over her lips. 'Now you see why it has to be put with . . . the other stuff.'

Travis carefully refolded the paper. When he went to put it back in the drawer, something caught his eye. 'What's this?'

'What?'

'Very tiny writing inside the drawer. I can't make out what it says.'

'Let me see.' She pulled a two-inch-wide magnifying glass from her purse.

'You just happen to have a magnifying glass?'

'Yeah,' she answered, her tone saying, *doesn't everyone?* 'You would carry one too after reading the fine print of about a thousand contracts from florists, and caterers and — '

'Okay. I get it. What does it say?'

'*For Laudine from Iwein, trapped in the land of his foes 1945 E. W.*'

'That seems to indicate he was a POW.'

Caroline handed the magnifying glass to Travis so he could see the inscription for himself. 'Probably, although there are other possibilities,' she said. 'Many POWs attended the crafts classes held at the camp to make gifts to send home, small items for their own use, and items to trade with other prisoners or sell for cash.'

'And you know this how?'

'Remember, I told you earlier that I researched the topic of POWs for some magazine articles I wrote.'

'Right. Well, it should be easy enough to check on a prisoner named Iwein.'

'Iwein is the name of a legendary knight,' said a deep voice from the doorway.

Travis replaced the map, slid the tiny drawer shut and stashed the eagle in his pocket. Fortunately, the service counter forestalled Karl Volker's entrance into the main room.

'May I help you?' Phyllis asked as she approached the stranger.

'I'm here to see Sheriff Beaumont,' Volker said, sliding a business card in her direction but nodding towards Travis to indicate that he already knew him. He plopped a file folder several inches think on the counter.

'It's okay, Phyllis. I've got it.'

The deputy returned to her post at the dispatch switchboard, but it was a slow day, so even though she put her headset on, it covered only one ear, and she sat facing the main office.

Travis stepped up to the counter. 'I know why you're here, but Judge Macky has already issued an injunction — '

'Yes, yes. I just came from there. He said

you would explain.'

That sounded about right. 'The injunction prevents any further disturbance of the body until the court can determine whether or not the mummy was a Native American.'

'Wouldn't that be easier to do with DNA testing?'

'Maybe. Not my call. Nothing disruptive can be done until we receive the okay.'

'When will that be?'

'Could be days, could be months. There's a case in Seattle that's been in the courts for twelve years.'

'All I'm asking for is a small bit of hair.'

'Sorry, not gonna happen.'

Volker was turning away when Caroline spoke up.

'Excuse me, but you look so familiar. Don't I know you?'

Volker shook his head, and Travis volunteered, 'You must have seen him last night at the cave site.'

'Noooo.' She scratched the back of her neck. 'I'm sure it's not that. Have you ever attended a Hollywood wedding?'

'No.'

'I give up, but it'll come to me eventually.'

'So when are you going back to Germany?' Travis asked.

'I'll be around for a few more days,' Volker

said. 'After travelling eight thousand nine hundred and twenty-six kilometres, I might as well see the sights.'

Travis sensed there was more that Volker was leaving unsaid. 'Yeah, you wouldn't want to come that far and leave without visiting the Giant Pistachio in Alamogordo.'

'Or the Alien Museum in Roswell,' Phyllis said.

Travis flashed her a glare.

Phyllis spun around in her chair and said, 'Haven Sheriff's Department. How may I help you?' even though the phone hadn't rung.

'What was it you were saying about Iwein, Mr Volker?' Caroline asked.

Travis understood she was trying to change the subject, but he didn't appreciate any encouragement for Volker to stick around.

'Call me Karl, please. Iwein is a figure from our medieval literature, often referred to as Middle High German. He is a knight, the protagonist of a poem by Hartmann von Aue circa 1197.'

'So that means whoever made . . . the person we're looking for was probably named after this knight,' Caroline said.

'Possibly,' Volker said. 'But I thought I also heard you say something about being imprisoned by his enemies, which would make sense, because in the poem Iwein cannot return to his love Laudine. Her inclusion convinces me that your inscription is a literary reference. Iwein and Laudine were star-crossed lovers.'

'You mean like Romeo and Juliet?' Travis asked, not wanting Volker to dominate Caroline's attention.

'More like Lancelot and Guinevere. The poem is part of a wide spectrum of Arthurian literature.'

Caroline's cell phone rang and she excused herself. 'Sorry, I have to take this.' She stepped away and turned her back.

'Well, if I hear anything on the injunction, I'll be sure to let you know,' Travis said, hoping Volker would leave.

Caroline ducked under the service counter. 'I totally lost track of time and now I'm going to be late.' She looked directly at Travis. 'I'll call you later.'

Excitement and promise lit her eyes, something he hadn't seen in a long time.

★ ★ ★

Bev Frye, the housekeeper, answered the Petersens' door with a lack of warmth to match the rush of cold air escaping the open door. 'Ms Enid is expecting you.'

Caroline nodded formally, wondering what

was going on. 'I'm so sorry I'm late,' she said to Enid as soon as she saw her.

'I understand, and I appreciate your call.' She looked around almost fearfully. 'Perhaps we should get started immediately.'

Caroline placed a fourteen-by-eleven piece of foam core on the coffee table. She'd already pasted pictures of a few items on the board: tents, chairs and tables with white coverings, and the portable wooden dance floor. 'In these folders I have pictures of various options. We can add items to the collage as we step through the plans and we'll end up with a visual representation that shows how everything fits together.'

Enid nodded eagerly.

'Here's a mock-up of your invitation. Standard. Formal. I chose the off-white with a bevel edge.'

'It's perfect.'

Caroline used a glue stick to paste the invitation in the upper left corner of the collage. She paused, took a deep breath, and blew it out. 'You said you wanted colour, so I thought gerbera daisies would be the main flower.' She showed Enid a picture of a bright bouquet.

'Oh I love that.'

Caroline pasted the picture in the middle of the collage.

'The girls are thrilled to be included, but Jurgen mentioned that maybe four attendants is a bit much for a reaffirmation ceremony. He doesn't want people saying we're pretentious.'

After holding a full-scale wedding with a sit-down dinner and live band for two hundred people, who would possibly say that?

'They're family,' Caroline said. 'Some might call it pretentious if you excluded them. I thought their dresses could be the same colours as the gerbera daisies in your bouquet.' She spread out a handful of flower cut-outs.

'That's funny. I used to colour-coordinate everything when the girls were little; Bindie was always yellow, Tilly blue, Elsie green, and Suzanne pink.'

'Then those are the colours we'll use.'

'But not pastel. I want bold, vibrant colours.'

'Let's go for golden yellow, turquoise blue, deep lime green, and a really saturated pink.' Caroline picked out a flower of each colour, dabbed the back with the glue stick and grouped them together in the lower right-hand corner of the collage.

'What about the grandchildren?'

'Hmmm. What if we dress them in white and make their accessories, like hair bows, belts or sashes, the colour of their mother's dress?'

'And bow ties for the little boys.'

'Very cute. Then we could use red for all the accents — table runners, napkins, vases, ribbons, that sort of stuff — to tie everything all together.'

'Perfect. I love red.'

Caroline pasted in place by the tables and chairs the red linens and centrepiece vases. 'What do you think?'

'I love it.'

'I hear a *but* in your voice.'

'It looks a little casual. Jurgen wants elegant and classic.'

Caroline looked at the collage for a few seconds. 'I have an idea.' She pulled off the picture of the vases and replaced it with a tall centrepiece with swags of pearls on it. 'We'll use strings of pearls as a unifying element. Nothing could be more classic and elegant.'

'But we can still have gold, turquoise, lime and pink?'

'Hmmm. Let's see. The biggest grouping of colour will be the bridesmaid's dresses. We'll make sure they have simple lines like elegant evening fashions of the forties. And I know exactly where to find them: Eugenia's Classic Creations.'

Enid covered her mouth but couldn't

prevent a giggle from escaping. 'Eugenia hasn't updated her styles for fifty years.'

'And that makes her shop perfect. Does each of the girls have a pearl necklace to wear?'

'I don't think so, but I'll go to the jeweller tomorrow and purchase four matching strands of pearls, my gift to them for standing up with me.

'Perfect. We'll make your bouquet mostly white roses with pops of colour rather than all gerbera daisies.'

'And the girls can carry white daisies.'

'Daisies aren't really a formal flower. How about lilies?'

'To me lilies are for funerals. And everyone knows daisies are my favourite flower,' Enid said, pointing to her flower earrings.

'Daisies it is.' Caroline found pictures of white roses and daisies in her folder and pasted them on the collage. Then she held the board up so Enid could see it better.

'Excellent. It might not be what Jurgen envisioned, but it's exactly what I'd hoped for.'

'Who do you have in mind to officiate?'

'We've already talked to the minister at our church.'

'Excellent. We're moving right along. Now, I know you wanted a live band, but I could only find one that plays swing music. They're expensive, but they do come highly recommended.' She gave Enid a brochure and some pages she'd printed off the night before. 'They're available on your date and this is their play list. If you'd like to hear them before signing . . . '

'That won't be necessary. I think we went to a charity function where they played. Besides, if they're the only band, what choice do we have?'

'A DJ would play recordings of the original artists.'

'No, I'd rather have live music. Records are great, but there's no substitute for a real band.'

'I agree.' Caroline added a picture of the band, all dressed in tuxes, that she'd also printed from their website.

Enid set the play list to one side. 'I'm going to ask Jurgen to choose the music.'

'Great idea. Now, about the menu. Since certain foods, like butter and sugar, were still rationed in 1946 . . . '

'On the farm we had it easier than the townies. We churned our own butter, and kept bees.'

'I talked to Lewis Warner.'

'Maybelle's grandson? I heard he was back in town. Isn't he some sort of famous chef?'

'He's amazing. And he's actually excited about using vintage recipes and keeping within the rationing parameters. Said it would be healthy and have plenty of choices for those on a limited diet, like vegetarian or low-carb. I recommend we go with him, but I can get bids from other caterers if you want. It's up to you.'

'I trust your judgement. We were quite inventive cooks back then. I remember my Aunt Helen made a Crazy Cocoa Cake that called for vinegar and oil rather than eggs. She made it special for me every Sunday. I loved that cake.' Enid sighed. 'Oh my, that really brings back memories.'

'Maybelle gave Lewis dozens of recipes for things like Mock Goose, False Fish, Woolton Pie, and a War Cake made with no eggs and no milk.' Caroline really wanted Enid to go for the idea. 'I think it sounds fun. Unusual, and in keeping with our theme.'

'Definitely what a wedding in 1946 would have served. Let's do it.'

'Wonderful. I'll call Lewis, and we should have a full menu for you to review by tomorrow.'

'No corn. I guess they only had field corn in Germany, because Jurgen absolutely refuses to eat what he calls pig food.'

Caroline didn't know what to say to that,

other than 'I'll make a note.'

As if the mention of his name had summoned him, Jurgen marched into the room.

'So you finally showed up,' he said. Obviously he wasn't happy about Caroline's delayed arrival.

'Jurgen had an appointment to meet the vet in the barn and couldn't wait for you,' Enid explained.

Caroline, no stranger to the power plays of the rich and famous, refused to be bullied by a martinet. She stood up so that she wouldn't be apologizing from the subservient position.

'I'm sorry I missed you. I do understand that previous commitments must be honoured.' By making it sound like she was late for the same reason he wasn't available, she levelled the playing field. Then she stuck out her hand, thus putting her in the one-up position. His only choice, short of complete rudeness, was to shake her hand and thereby de facto accept her apology. Her risky manoeuvre paid off.

He gestured for her to be seated and then took his place in the big leather chair.

'We've made a lot of progress on the wedding plans,' Enid said in a small voice.

Ignoring his wife, Jurgen turned to Caroline. 'You are the woman on the mummy video,' he said in an accusing tone. 'I did not recognize you at first due to the white hat.'

'Yes.' Hopefully lots of other people had had that same problem. And if she were really lucky, lots of other people would think she was wearing a hat rather than a gauze turban. She picked up the band's song list and handed it to him. 'You can schedule the music to your liking, or you can just designate a few special tunes for specific dances and the bandleader can — '

'Let him do the job I'm paying him to do.' Jurgen waved off any concern with the music. 'What is the status with the mummy? Did they confirm he was located on my land, or are they still insisting it's federal land?'

'I'm not sure. I think he was found on the edge of the White Sands Missile Range, but you really should check with Sheriff Beaumont.'

Jurgen waggled his finger at Enid. 'It's that strip of land, that same strip of land.' He turned back to Caroline. 'Where did they take the mummy?'

'You'll have to talk to the sheriff about that.

'Do they have any identification yet?'

Caroline shook her head. 'Again, you need to talk — '

'Do they know why he was mummified instead of rotting away?'

'Jurgen!' Enid said.

'This is important.'

'Caroline is here to talk about the wedding, not some silly mummy,' Enid insisted.

'You don't understand,' he said, leaning forward in his chair. 'This could change everything.'

'How? It's no business of ours.'

'They found gold. You'll see how much it concerns us when the treasure hunters start arriving. No respect for fences, property ownership, or anything else.' He sat back and waved his arms wildly. 'They'll be every-where.'

'I don't care. If it doesn't have to do with the wedding, it will just have to wait.'

Enid might just as well have stomped her foot. Apparently she could stand up to her husband if pushed far enough. Caroline wanted to say *you go, girl* but opted for silence after seeing the daggers shooting between the couple.

Jurgen suddenly stood and marched into an adjoining room that appeared to be his office, slamming the door shut.

'Now, where were we?' Enid asked in her usual sweet voice, as if they had never been interrupted.

Caroline was still flummoxed by Jurgen's over-the-top reaction. 'I . . . I . . . '

'Please excuse my husband. He's very frustrated over that particular piece of land.

He's been trying to prove ownership for decades. The government will never let it go now.'

'Oh. Well, I think we were just about to wrap things up for today. I'll get back to you with the contracts for the band, florist, rentals and caterer.'

'I'll be in town tomorrow morning, so I'll stop by your office.'

'If you have time, we could go over to Eugenia's and talk to her about the bridesmaids' dresses. Would any of your daughters be available to go with us?'

'I'll ask them.'

'Okay, I'll call for an appointment and let you know later today when it's scheduled.'

'Can we make it in the evening? With jobs and families, daytime is problematic for the girls.'

'I'm sure Eugenia will understand and stay open late if necessary.' For the sale of four custom dresses, the struggling shopkeeper would probably keep the doors unlocked until midnight.

★　★　★

When Caroline finally returned to her car, she heaved a sigh of relief, letting the tension of the appointment dissipate. This was turning into a job that rivalled a Hollywood wedding in terms of unpleasant surprises. And she was only two days into it.

What else could possibly happen?

She could almost hear Mimi's voice saying, 'Don't ever say that! You're inviting disaster.'

As she drove back to her office, she made a mental list of everything she had to do that afternoon: contracts, dresses, and oh yeah, call Travis. She couldn't forget that.

6

All Caroline wanted was a nice quiet afternoon so that she could tie up loose ends on the wedding plans. She'd decorated her little shop in the spirit of a Victorian parlour, with comfortable sofas and chairs arranged in conversational groupings. She could seat a wedding party of ten if necessary. Her whitewashed desk was angled in the far corner so she could see the door but not be facing it.

She drew up a preliminary layout of the venue. Then she booked three extra-large tents, twenty-five round tables, a long table for the head table, and food service, linen and the portable dance floor, all from Rent-A-Party in El Paso.

While that contract came in on the fax machine, she was able to book the band. When she notified the bandleader that he would be given carte blanche for the music choices, he strongly suggested that the couple choose at least the song for the first dance. Caroline went out on a limb and chose 'String of Pearls' for Enid. He promised that a contract would be faxed within the hour.

The tinkling of the bell over the shop door interrupted her just as she dialled the phone number of Eugenia's Classic Creations. As soon as she saw who had entered, she terminated the phone call and pasted a smile on her face as she walked towards the door.

'Good afternoon, Mrs Stanley, Mr Stanley,' she said. Gloria was alone, of course, her husband having passed away some thirty or so years ago, before Caroline was even born. But since she had always spoken as if Mr Stanley were at her side, everyone else did the same. 'What an unexpected pleasure.'

Not. But Caroline just couldn't be rude. Actually she should have expected Gloria Stanley sooner rather than later. The biggest gossip in Haven had not retained her crown for decades without actively pursuing her supply of news. Unable to avoid the inevitable, the trick was to give her as little information as possible.

'Hello, my dear.' Gloria sat down in the corner of a mauve brocade love seat.

'Can I get you anything? A cold drink? A cup of tea?'

'We don't want to put you to any trouble.'

'No trouble. I was just about to fix something for myself.'

'A small glass of sweet tea would be welcome.'

'I'll be right back.' Caroline slipped through the door to the back room where, in addition to storage shelves, there was a small kitchenette. After putting ice in three tall crystal glasses, she filled them with sweet tea and placed them on a silver tray lined with a hand-tatted doily. She added pristine white napkins trimmed with a tiny edge of lace. All items she'd found at the church's missionary sale.

She took the last six lemon meringue cookies out of a big poinsettia-decorated tin, placed them on a pink glass plate, and added them to the tray with a sigh. But was it relief or regret? Mimi had given her a supply of her favourite cookies to serve to clients. The problem was, there had been too few clients and the bright red tin was too accessible. Caroline had eaten dozens of the cookies over the last three weeks.

Pasting another smile on her face, she served the Stanleys and took a seat on the twin sofa. 'So, what has brought you downtown today?'

'We came to see Sheriff Beaumont, but apparently he's out chasing bad guys with that Indian cop.' Gloria paused and tilted her head as if listening to a voice no one else could hear. 'Yes. Of course, you're right,' she said to the air on her right, and then turned to Caroline. 'Mr Stanley reminded me that the correct term is now Native American. We do try to keep up with the times, but at our age it's not easy.'

'I think it's wonderful that you make the effort.' Conversation with Gloria was like a competitive racquetball match. Position in relation to the ball was key. Caroline settled back on the sofa, waiting for her opponent to make the next conversational volley.

Gloria sipped and nibbled and dabbed at her lips with her napkin. 'I'm going to,' she said over her shoulder through clenched teeth. Then she smiled sweetly at Caroline. 'How is your business doing?'

'Fine.'

'I knew we needed a wedding planner right here in Haven. You've found the suppliers in the area as good as you did in Hollywood?'

'I've been pleased with everyone's work.'

'Oh? Who does your printing?'

'I've been sending everything to Belmonte's in El Paso.'

'Hmmm, yes, they do have a good reputation.'

Caroline was totally at a loss as to where the conversation was headed. Not a good feeling. Especially with Gloria. 'Why do you ask?'

Gloria put down her glass and dabbed at

her lips again. 'I'm not usually one to put myself forward,' she said, slapping at something off to her right without looking in that direction. 'You may know that Mr Stanley and I ran the newspaper for many years, until we retired and our son took over. But you may not know that we also did a number of printing jobs on the side.'

'Really?'

'Yes. Well, lately our investments haven't been paying back as well as in the past . . .'

'Please, I . . .'

'We've been taking on a few select jobs, using our contacts to print business cards, invitations, announcements, that sort of thing.'

Caroline had let her attention wander until she heard the word 'invitations'. She sat up straighter. 'How fast can you turn a job around?'

'Suitably compensated, twenty-four hours.'

'Do you have an addressing service?'

'Mr Stanley and I do the calligraphy ourselves. We each won the penmanship prize in sixth grade, me four years after him. Our handwriting is identical, perfect Palmer Method.'

Caroline went to her desk and pulled out the guest list for the Petersen wedding. Mostly couples, a few that included children, and a few single names with a *plus guest* notation. 'Roughly one hundred and ten invitations. I guess I'll order one-fifty to allow for mistakes.'

'One-twenty-five to allow for keepsakes. We don't make errors.'

'How long? Absolute minimum.'

'Three days after delivery from the printer.'

'For a price?'

'I've always said, properly compensated is properly motivated.'

Caroline could not believe she was doing this, even as she opened her mouth and said, 'If you can bring me a contract by tomorrow . . .'

'We have one right here,' Gloria said, opening her large purse and pulling out a manila folder. 'I'll just fill in a few blanks and we're all set.'

After coming to an agreement, Gloria, and presumably Mr Stanley, left the salon. Caroline returned to her desk, a bit dazed by the speed at which the town's biggest gossip had morphed from a nuisance into a life-saving business supplier. She could only hope half of the invitations weren't addressed in invisible ink.

Paul and Nina Bennett came over from their flower shop next door. In the Pink was a family business Paul had inherited from his parents.

'Hey, who's minding your store?' Caroline asked as she hugged each of her friends.

Paul waved off her concern. 'It's the afternoon doldrums. Business won't pick up until school's out. I have got to know what the Gossip Queen wanted.'

'That from the Prince of Tittle-tattle. I, however, came to see if you like your new window design.' Nina fluffed a swag made of fine net. 'I think it needs a little something-something.'

'It's perfect,' Paul said to his wife before turning back to Caroline. 'Come on, don't make me beg.'

'I bet you say that to all the girls,' she said.

'Not any more,' Nina answered for him. 'I got him roped, saddled and broke to the bit.'

'Hold on there, cowgirl,' Paul said. 'There's still some bucking left in this bronco.'

'Okay, you two. That's enough. Shoo. Go back to your own shop and let me get some work done,' Caroline said with a laugh. 'And for the record, Gloria Stanley didn't tell me anything,' she called after them.

Caroline cleaned up the dishes and settled back at her desk. She set up a seven o'clock appointment with Eugenia and left a message on Enid's voicemail about the time. She sent Lewis a long email about the no-corn menu for the sit-down dinner, closing with a request that a contract be faxed to her before ten the following morning.

Then she paused with her hand on the phone. She realized she'd done everything else first as a way of avoiding the promised call to Travis. It wasn't as if they didn't have anything to talk about, just that they never seemed to have time to talk about important issues, like what had gone wrong with their marriage.

She flipped open her cell phone and scrolled down the contacts until she came to his name. She'd added his cell number off the list posted by Mimi's kitchen phone even though she'd never intended to use it, and had even lied to Phyllis about having it. Before she changed her mind, she pressed the call button.

Strangely, the ringing sounded like the bell over her door. Then she realized it *was* her door. She flipped the phone shut and stood up, hiding her hands in her pockets, feeling somehow guilty, like a kid caught with contraband candy.

'Mimi? Lou? What are you doing here?'

'Well! That's a nice welcome,' Mimi said.

'I'm just surprised, that's all.'

Lou wheeled her highly decorated walker past her friend and plopped down on the chair closest to the door. 'It's hot as Hades out there and I knew you'd have your air cranked up ... or should that be cranked down?'

'We thought we might take a little breather before finishing our walk.'

'I'll get you something to drink,' Caroline said, heading for the back room.

'Just some water,' Mimi called. 'Bottles if you have them. We still have to go three more times around the town square.'

Lou groaned.

'I thought you two walked early in the morning while it's still cool,' Caroline said. She brought in three bottles of water and three glasses with ice, because she'd never seen her grandmother drink directly from a bottle.

But Mimi surprised her by taking a healthy swig. 'Ah, nice and cold.'

Lou also accepted a bottle. 'The water in the drinking fountain next to the courthouse is the same temperature as the sidewalk.'

'We decided to take our walk late because we have appointments at Dixie May's Cut'n' Curl.'

'Probably not our best idea,' Lou added. 'The walking late, not the getting our hair cut.' She ran her hand through the hair at the back of her neck, which had thinned quite a bit, whether with age or her condition. Illness hadn't affected Mimi's thick silver hair, at least not yet.

Mimi looked at her watch. 'We'd better get along.'

'My get along has done got up and gone.'

'Come on,' Mimi said, offering Lou a hand. 'We'll do one more circuit around the square real slow.'

'One?' Lou brightened right up.

'We'll make up the distance tomorrow morning.'

'Ugh.' Lou groaned as she stood.

Was Lou protesting standing or the prospect of extra walking?

'There's something else,' Mimi said, pinching her ear lobe as if the action would help her remember. After a moment she threw up her hands and shook her head. 'What did I forget?' she asked Lou.

'I can't even remember what I was supposed to remind you about.'

Caroline followed them to the door. 'Well, if either of you recall whatever it was, I'll probably be here at least another hour.' Then she remembered she still had an article on making cheese to finish. 'Probably closer to two hours. Hey, maybe I can give you two a ride home.'

'That's it,' Lou said, spinning her walker around towards Mimi and blocking the door.

'I was supposed to remind you to call Caroline to see if she could give us a ride because Travis . . . '

'Is out on a case,' Mimi finished in a triumphant tone. She turned to Caroline.

'Sure, but let's talk either inside or out, not stand here with the door open letting out all the cooled air.'

Lou backed up, stumbling in her haste and nearly falling into a passer-by, who caught her and set her back on her feet.

'Oh my.' Lou turned and looked up at the tall blond stranger. 'Thank you, sir.'

'Are you all right?'

'I'm fine. You?'

He laughed, and that was when Caroline stepped around the other women. 'It's you,' he said, reaching out to her with an open hand. 'You are the friend of the sheriff, no?'

'Acquaintance,' Caroline corrected as she shook his hand.

'Sorry. I do not know this word.' He pulled a small notebook out of his pocket and made a notation.

'It means we know each other but we're less than friendly,' she said.

'You know this man?' Lou asked.

'We met this morning at the courthouse.' She introduced Karl Volker. 'Karl came all the way from Germany to see if Poor Fred,

120

the mummy, is his grandfather.'

'To prove the fact as I know it is true,' he said, 'all I need is a DNA test.'

'Unfortunately for Karl, the Apache nation has an injunction against any further disturbance of the mummy in order to provide time to prove he's Native American,' Caroline explained.

'So what are you going to do now?' Mimi asked him.

'I am looking for options but I haven't found any. So for the next few days I'm a tourist. Perhaps you could direct me to a place to get an authentic American meal.'

'Maybelle's,' Caroline said.

'That's where I had my midday repast. I was hoping for somewhere different. I've been craving a really good burger, not fast food though.'

'You could drive to El Paso. They must have a thousand restaurants,' Caroline said.

'Or you could come to my house for dinner.'

'Mimi!' Caroline could not believe her grandmother was inviting a total stranger into her home.

'We're grilling tonight, cheeseburgers and hot dogs. Can't get more American than that.'

'I'm flabbergasted by your generous invitation. I would be honoured.' He clicked his heels together and bowed.

'Then it's settled.' Mimi looked at her watch. 'Well, we must rush off . . . '

'Yeah, we have to get to the Cut'n'Curl before Dixie gets her panties in a twist.'

'But if you'll meet us right here at five o'clock, my granddaughter will drive us all home.'

They said their farewells, Mimi bussed Caroline's cheek, and Lou blew her a kiss.

'May I escort you to your appointment?' Karl asked, holding one arm out to Mimi while keeping his other hovering protectively behind Lou.

The two older women giggled girlishly as they walked away, and Caroline rolled her eyes. Then she whipped her phone out of her pocket and had dialled Travis before she'd even made it back inside. She was tempted to hang up the second she heard his voice, but with the latest surprising development, she wanted him to show up at Mimi's for dinner too. She only got his voicemail, so she had to settle for leaving a message.

While she waited for his call back, she finished her article and organized everything for her next meeting with Enid.

★ ★ ★

'How are the plans for the Petersen ceremony going?'

'Good.' Caroline answered her grandmother without turning away from the sink, where she was cubing the potatoes Mimi had baked the previous day. Many cooks boiled the potatoes for potato salad but Mimi's recipe called for cold baked spuds, cut-up hard-boiled eggs, finely chopped celery, green pepper, red pepper, diced dill pickles, mustard, mayonnaise, and her secret ingredient, a generous splash of Tabasco sauce. She usually covered the bowl and let the salad sit for several hours in the fridge to meld the flavours, but tonight there wasn't time.

That reminded Caroline that Lewis was collecting recipes from the war years. She asked Mimi if she remembered any.

'I wasn't much of a cook in 1946,' Mimi said. 'I was only ten years old, you know.'

'Do you remember Nana making anything in particular?'

'No, but her notebooks are in the bottom drawer of the buffet in the dining room. I'll look and see if she wrote down any wartime recipes. There's always Mock Apple Pie, made with Ritz crackers.'

'Did they exist back then?' Caroline mixed all the ingredients of the potato salad together.

'Sure, we loved taking Ritz crackers and peanut butter in our school lunches. Mock

Apple Pie was also made with soda crackers or saltines, that dated back to before the Civil War. But the Ritz recipe seems to be the most popular. You know, I think we have all the ingredients. Let's make a Mock Apple Pie.'

'Why? You already made a regular one.'

'That's why it's so perfect. We can have a taste test. It'll be fun.'

Caroline glanced out the window at her brothers trying to teach Karl baseball. 'We do have a guest.'

'Don't you think Karl would find it interesting?'

She looked out the window again. Karl swung at an easy pitch and missed it by a mile. 'Maybe you're right. He's not doing all that well with baseball.'

By the time Lou arrived from next door, fresh from her forced rest period, the kitchen smelled of cinnamon and nutmeg.

'I love the smell of apple pie baking,' she said.

Mimi and Caroline looked at each other and giggled.

'What?' Lou spread her hands and looked down. 'Did I forget to put on my jeans again?'

'No, dear. You look lovely.' Mimi patted her friend's shoulder and led her to a seat at the table in the alcove. She explained about the contest. 'You can be one of our tasters.'

'That fake pie doesn't stand a chance. I've been a judge at the county fair for the last five years,' Lou added in an aside to Caroline.

'We'll see,' Mimi said. She went to the door and called for Bobby Ray to put the burgers on the grill and Bobby Lee to come help bring stuff from the kitchen to the patio table.

'Of course you'll have coffee with the pie,' Lou said, her voice hopeful.

'You'll have decaf,' Mimi replied without looking up from the tomato she was slicing.

'Drat. You know that stuff tastes like horse piss.'

'We've been over this a thousand times. The doctor said you aren't — '

'That young whippersnapper doesn't understand the big picture. Decent coffee is a quality of life issue.'

'Regardless, Travis made me promise I wouldn't help you cheat any more.'

'It's so unfair. You don't have a restricted diet, or mandatory exercise, or a regulated bedtime, and you're the one who's dying . . . Oops. I'm sorry, Mimi. Sometimes my mouth . . . Please forgive me.'

Mimi gave her a stern look. 'No harm done this time, because Caroline and I have already talked about . . . it. But please, as my dearest friend, don't mention it again. None of the other children know.'

'Maybe we should. Talk about it, I mean,' Caroline said, hoping to capitalize on an opportunity to learn more about Mimi's condition.

'You said it yourself earlier, we have a guest. And besides that, dinner is nearly ready. Everyone grab something to carry out to the deck. Lou, you can take this bag with paper plates and napkins and plastic silverware.'

'I see we're in full picnic mode,' Lou said, looping the long handles of the carryall over her head. 'My kind of entertaining,' she added before making her way outside.

'We could use real dishes,' Caroline said.

'Why? To impress a man who lives halfway around the world and whom we'll probably never see again?'

'Then why ask him over?'

'Hopefully he has some interesting dinner conversation.'

'Are you saying we're boring?'

'Not at all, dear. I love hearing about your weddings, the people Bobby Lee arrests, and Bobby Ray's ministry. It's just that from time to time it's nice to talk about different things, broaden one's horizons.'

'Travis asked you to pump Karl for information, didn't he?'

Mimi bit her lip and turned away.

126

'I knew it.'

'He simply asked that if Lou and I learned anything interesting to pass it along.'

'Uh huh. Knowing the two of you would then ask leading questions. No one would suspect the interest of two sweet elderly women who are interested because . . . why?'

'All men like to think they're fascinating to women, no matter their age.'

'Age of the men or the women?'

'Both.'

'I'm not sure this is a good idea.'

'Or are you jealous because Travis didn't ask you?'

'What didn't Travis ask you?' Bobby Lee said as he bounded through the door. 'Mmm, smells like heaven in here. Lou told us about the contest. Count me in. Any job that guarantees two pieces of pie is right as rain with me.'

Caroline handed him the big bowl of potato salad and a basket of condiments, thankful that he'd been distracted by pie.

He paused at the door and turned. 'You can go stag to the harvest dance at the country club,' he said to his sister. 'They always play plenty of group dances.'

She stuck her tongue out at him.

'And in case you forgot, the *old maids* tend to sit along the left wall.'

She threw the dishtowel in his direction.

'Mutual corners,' Mimi said, as she used to do when they were kids. She didn't have to raise her voice. They both knew the signal that she'd had enough and it was time to retreat.

Bobby Lee left whistling 'Single Lady'.

★   ★   ★

Dinner conversation was the ordinary chit-chat expected at a table of strangers. With Lou and Mimi tag-teaming questions, they learned that Karl's English was so good because he had attended the Odegard School of Aerospace Sciences at the University of North Dakota for a year on an exchange programme, that he was on their cross-country ski team, and that he'd lived with a German family in Grand Forks.

Lou drew out the information on the business Karl owned, a company that manufactured parts for supersonic, super-secret aircraft. Mimi asked about his family: divorced, twice, two sons, Karl Jr, fourteen, and Oswald, age ten, both in private school.

Caroline forced herself to not keep looking at the door, but she wondered where Travis could be. She'd left him a message and assumed he would come to dinner to be assured of their safety if nothing else. She sent up a prayer that his tardiness didn't mean he'd been hurt, a worry always in the back of her mind.

The blind apple pie testing was a big hit. Among much laughter and teasing, Karl surprised everyone by being the only one who correctly identified the genuine article. He thought the Ritz Mock Apple Pie tasted like lemon.

Bobby Ray excused himself. He had several updates to make to his website and he wanted to have everything in order before opening his virtual doors to those in need of spiritual counselling during the darkest hours.

Mimi decided to serve a choice of decaf coffee, hot chocolate or beer at the fire pit in the garden. The once dirt sometimes muddy path had been covered with a boardwalk, an irregular pattern of stairs and landings that meandered down the hill. Bobby Lee built a fire in the large copper pit. The flames warded off the chill of after-dark in the desert clime, and the surrounding log benches and flat rocks created a cosy, intimate setting.

'Tell us about your grandfather,' Mimi said softly.

Karl was seated on a log bench next to Caroline and across the fire from Lou and Mimi, while Bobby Lee stood near the fire adding logs and stoking it higher.

Karl leaned forward, rested his elbows on his knees and dangled his half-empty beer bottle between two fingers. 'Which one do you want to hear about? The hero of my childhood, or the one I only learned existed a few weeks ago?'

'Both, I should think.'

'When I was a child, my parents worked long hours; Vater was a surgeon and Mutter is an architect. Come to think of it, she still works sixty hours a week even though she keeps talking about scaling back and retiring soon.'

'What does your mother think of you searching for your grandfather?' Caroline asked.

'Not much. Her stance is that people hide things for a reason and no good comes from ferreting out secrets better left alone.'

'I disagree,' Lou said. 'Honesty is always best in the long run.'

'I'm not so sure,' Mimi said. 'Sometimes the truth is just too hurtful.'

'I take it you're looking for your paternal grandfather,' Caroline said to Karl to get the conversation back on the information-gathering track.

'Yes. Oma lived in a small cottage at the edge of our garden and I stayed with her whenever my parents were away. I don't remember living anywhere else, but she told me the family was once very poor. She grew up in a hut with a dirt floor. They brought the livestock into the house during the winter for additional warmth.'

'You think that's poor?' said Lou. 'When I was growing — '

'We are not trading poor stories,' Mimi said, her voice firm. 'This is Karl's turn to talk.'

'No, I would love to hear someone else — ' Karl too was cut off.

'Do not encourage her. Even though you may not have heard her wild yarns — '

'God's honest truth, every word.'

'But we've heard them many times,' Mimi finished.

Lou stuck out her bottom lip but remained silent. Bobby Lee excused himself and stepped to the other side of the garden, putting his cell to his ear. Caroline hoped it was Travis calling him. She was no longer worried about the stranger in their midst, but Travis's continued absence was producing more than a little anxiety. She didn't say anything because she didn't want to upset Lou.

She turned to Karl. 'So, you spent a lot of time with your grandmother. I can relate to

131

that. Mimi took care of us during the school year so we didn't have to ride the bus all the way in from the ranch. I'm sure your grandmother was a big influence on you.'

Karl chuckled. 'In ways my parents didn't anticipate or appreciate.'

'What do you mean?'

'According to Oma, after the war few people wanted to be associated with the losers. Suddenly known Nazi sympathizers claimed to have been secretly working for the resistance all along. She was fond of saying that if the resistance had had that many members, there would have been no one at the front to meet the Allies.'

'My father said the same about the French,' Lou said.

'Even though Oma was horrified by what Hitler had done, she was still proud of her heritage. She filled me with heroic stories and epic poems: Attila, Hagen, Beowulf, Wiglaf, Sigmund the dragon slayer. And there were wonderful stories of my grandfather, the poor farm boy who saved his unit from snipers, took a machine-gun nest practically single-handed, and stopped a rampaging tank with only six men and a handful of grenades. He came to Rommel's attention by killing two hundred and forty of the enemy and capturing a hundred and thirty-two more. He learned Arabic and joined Rommel's staff as a translator before being killed by stepping in front of the general and taking the bullet meant for him. I came to think of my grandfather as another Wolfhart, a supreme warrior who, as he lay dying on the battlefield, told his uncle not to mourn him, for he died with great honour.'

'Hard for a mere mortal to live up to mythical standards,' Mimi said.

'Not if you create it all with stolen details, as I found out much later. Apparently Oma was not above appropriating the deeds of other heroes, including Americans like Alvin York and Audie Murphy.'

'I thought some of that sounded familiar,' Lou said.

'Not to me,' Caroline admitted.

'Looks like we need to rent the old movies *Sergeant York* and *To Hell and Back*,' Mimi said.

'That must be where Oma learned their stories. She loved American movies, especially Westerns. Randolph Scott and Jimmy Stewart were her favourites.'

'Didn't Jimmy Stewart play Sergeant York?' Lou asked.

'Gary Cooper,' Mimi said.

'Ah, yes.'

'I always said that man could have put his

boots beneath my bed anytime.'

'Mimi!' Caroline was shocked by the implication.

'What? You think you young people invented — '

'No,' Caroline said, a bit louder than she expected. Please, please don't say *romping in the hay, doing the duvet tango, mattress wrestling* or any other of Mimi's cute euphemisms. 'Why don't we get back to our guest's story?'

'I was going to say *being star-struck*,' Mimi said to Caroline out of the side of her mouth.

'I don't mind,' Karl said.

But either he was sitting a little too close to the fire, or he was blushing.

7

'When did you find out your grandmother was . . . um, elaborating on the truth?' Caroline asked, shifting closer to the fire pit. She was starting to feel chilled but she was unwilling to leave and miss any of the story.

'About six months ago, Oma decided to move to an apartment in a managed facility where several of her friends live. I was helping her pack when she came across a cedar-lined strongbox of letters from Grossvater that she'd forgotten she'd kept.'

Caroline couldn't imagine not remembering something so meaningful, even if it had been more than fifty years, but both Mimi and Lou nodded in agreement.

'Sometimes going into my attic is like Christmas morning,' Mimi said.

'All I have to do is open the bottom drawer of any piece of furniture in my house,' Lou said.

'So she gave the letters to you?' Caroline asked Karl.

'To burn.'

'What?' All three women cried out in dismay.

'And that only after making me promise not to read them.'

'You didn't agree?' Caroline asked, appalled at the thought.

'Of course I did. As far as I knew they were love letters from their courtship. The thought of reading them made me slightly queasy.'

'But you didn't burn them,' Mimi said.

'As I was leaving the room to do her bidding, she called me back. She said she was worried about her immortal soul and had decided she didn't want to face her maker without correcting the lie she'd lived most of her life. That's when she told me her husband had not been killed in Africa but had surrendered with his unit and been a POW. For three years he'd written her every month. But at the end of the war, he didn't come home, and she never heard from him again.'

'Why didn't she try to find him?' Caroline asked.

'She did at first, but everything was so chaotic after the war, records haphazardly stored, many destroyed. One bureaucrat told her that based on the scant evidence available, his opinion was that Grossvater had opted to stay in America. She would have pursued it further, but that would have meant an expensive trip to Berlin where the records were kept. She had very little money and her first priority was to take care of her son. Eventually a friend helped her qualify for a widow's pension and she buried all thoughts of her now officially dead husband so deep she nearly began believing the lies herself.'

'But you started looking for him,' Mimi said.

'Not right away.'

'I'll bet she made you promise not to, not as long as she lived,' Lou said.

'You're right.'

Lou slapped her knee. 'I knew it.'

'Oma didn't want to know where he was buried if he was dead, and she didn't want to have anything to do with him if he wasn't. In fact she called him a few choice words I wasn't even aware she knew, much less thought would ever pass her lips.'

The women were silent; they all understood her reaction perfectly. Mimi was the first to speak. 'You are the same person you were before you knew she'd lied. Each of us is more than our heritage. We are the sum of our decisions. Yes, heritage can influence decisions, but it doesn't have to. By making up a heroic grandfather, even if he fought for the losing side, she gave you a personal legacy, so that you could honour the man if not all his actions.'

'Not so different from those who lied about

being involved with the resistance,' Lou said.

'The knowledge itself doesn't make you a different person. What you decide to do with that knowledge is what will truly affect you and possibly your sons and grandchildren.'

Karl stared into the dying fire with a thoughtful expression.

Caroline realized that the very fact that he was in Haven meant his grandmother had passed on. 'I'm sorry for your loss,' she said, her throat thickening. She knew she would be facing the same situation sooner rather than later. Ducking her head, she blinked furiously to stop the tears that threatened. When she glanced sideways to see if it was safe to wipe her eyes, Mimi was looking the other way. And Caroline noticed that her grandmother was shivering.

She jumped up. 'I'm going to run up to the house for a jacket. Please wait until I get back for the rest of your story,' she said to Karl. 'Does anyone else want a sweater?' she asked the group in general.

'There are some ponchos on the hooks by the kitchen door,' Mimi said. 'Would you bring a couple of those back with you?'

Caroline nodded, then turned and fled up the hill. As soon as she got out of the light of the fire she wiped at her eyes with her shirt. While she was up at the house she intended to find something to ease the indigestion caused by her anxiety. And maybe she would even give Phyllis a quick call just to make sure Travis was all right. No, that would send totally the wrong signal.

Unfortunately the same darkness that hid her tears also made it difficult to navigate the stairs. She stumbled, but a shadow swooped around her and prevented her from falling.

Her heartbeat spiked. 'Travis Henry Beaumont! You nearly scared the life outta me.' Why had her TB-radar failed to let her know he was near? She stepped back and slapped his hands away. 'And where have you been? I expected you for dinner after leaving you that message. Weren't you worried at all about Mimi inviting this stranger to her house? Did it never occur to you that maybe Lou might be in danger too?' Caroline couldn't stop the words coming out of her mouth, propelled as they were by frustration and worry. She bit her bottom lip and crossed her arms.

When she paused for breath, he said, 'Are you done?'

'Yes.'

'Was it good for you?'

Pressing her lips together to keep from smiling, she looked away. A quote from Marilyn Monroe about losing control came to mind: 'If you can't handle me at my worst, then you sure as hell don't deserve me at my best.' Travis always had seemed to sense when she needed room to vent.

She forced her shoulders to relax and the rest of her body did the same. 'Yes, thank you. I do feel better.' If not due to her tirade, then because she finally knew he was all right.

'I was on a stake-out when you called and had my phone turned off.'

'Why not just turn it to vibrate? What if your office needed to get a hold of you?'

'Out in the desert, sounds seem louder than normal and travel farther in the absence of ambient noise clutter like in a city. Even small sounds that don't belong to the area, like the whirring of a vibrating cell phone, stick out like a siren. And my staff know to send me a text if they reach voicemail.'

'My phone dings when I get a text.'

'I have that feature turned off.'

'But you need light to read.'

'A small light is easy enough to hide under a tarp or blanket.'

'I'm sorry I took off on a rant like that,' Caroline said, glad the dark hid her flaming cheeks.

'Even after I received your message I couldn't get away, but I'd already checked on Volker's credentials, and beside that, Bobby

Ray and Bobby Lee are here.'

'Perfect if we want to form a prayer circle or play hacky-sack.'

'That was uncalled for. Either one of your brothers is more capable of protecting your grandmother than you give them credit for.'

'Maybe. Okay, yes.' She just didn't want to admit to him that she felt safest when he was around. When she'd decided to remain in Haven to help Mimi, she'd known she would have to deal with Travis. Eventually. But she'd avoided him because she needed time to come to terms with everything she'd recently learned. Like they'd never been legally married, because the justice of the peace across the border who performed the ceremony wasn't licensed to do so. And Travis had claimed that the reason she'd left him, because he'd not been around when she'd needed him the most, wasn't fair. He might not have gone on that motorcycle trip if he'd known she was pregnant and then he would have been with her during the trauma of the miscarriage. She realized she'd made an illogical decision when her vulnerable emotions were under tremendous stress and then had been locked into that mindset. Could she get past that now? She wanted to try.

'So did you catch your bad guys?' she

asked, mostly to keep the conversation going.

'Not tonight, but we'll get them eventually.'

Caroline was confused. If Bobby Lee was down by the fire pit and Phyllis was at the station . . . 'You said *we*. You and Harlan were on a stake-out?'

Travis coughed, but it sounded suspiciously like he'd covered a sharp bark of laughter. 'I'm working with the tribal police force on this one. Miguel and I were watching a makeshift runway that we think is being used by drug smugglers.'

'Dangerous?'

'Boring.'

'But chasing drug smugglers is hazardous?'

'Can be. At times.'

She wrapped her arms around her body.

'Are you cold? Do you want my jacket?' He slipped his coat off even as he asked.

'Oh, no.' Caroline, who had suddenly remembered her original errand, spun and ran towards the house.

'Hey, what did I say now?' He scratched the back of his neck. He'd never met a more confusing woman than Caroline.

'Travis? Is that you, dear?'

He turned at the sound of his grandmother's voice. Lou made her way slowly up the boardwalk, Bobby Lee at her side. He carried a big flashlight aimed at the ground in front of her. Mimi and Karl followed.

'Hello. I was just coming down to the fire pit to join you.'

'We decided to make a fresh pot of *decaf* coffee,' Lou said with a comical grimace.

'That's my girl,' Travis said. He greeted everyone, kissed Mimi and Lou on the cheek and shook hands with Karl before taking Bobby Lee's place at Lou's side. When the deputy made an attention-getting noise in his throat, Travis jerked his head to the side and said, 'Take off,' out of the corner of his mouth.

'Thanks, boss,' Bobby Lee said as he hurriedly handed over the flashlight. He doffed his hat to the ladies, and disappeared across the yard.

'That boy acts like he's late for a hot date,' Lou said in an amused voice.

'What was he hanging around here for?' Mimi said.

Lou gave Travis a calculating look. After signalling her to drop the topic by giving her a small shake of his head, he said over his shoulder, 'Guess his girlfriend had to work late.' He started the party moving towards the house. 'Hey, I heard there was apple pie for dessert. Any left?'

'Plenty.' Mimi explained about the tasting contest.

'Count me in,' Travis said.

'I wonder if the pies taste different now that they've completely cooled,' Karl said.

Mimi chuckled. 'Is that a way of saying you want another piece?'

'Oh no, I was just thinking out loud about the test results.'

'You mean you *don't* want more pie?'

'I didn't say that either.'

As Travis opened the door to the kitchen, Caroline was exiting the house.

'I was just on my way back,' she said.

'We decided to make fresh coffee and have more pie while Karl finishes his story,' Mimi said, shooing everyone inside and to the table in the alcove.

'There's not much more to tell,' Karl said, taking the seat she indicated.

While Mimi ground the coffee beans and set up the drip pot, Caroline dished up pie, putting two slim pieces on one plate for Travis.

'Don't forget the blindfold,' Lou said.

'Now wait a minute.' Travis wasn't fond of not having all his senses available. Probably a major reason why he'd never really gotten into drugs or alcohol like some of the motorcycle buddies of his youth.

'It's okay, cowboy,' Caroline said as she sauntered towards him. 'You're safe here.'

She leaned close as she tied the bandanna around his head, her scent and nearness a heady combination. 'You know what they say?'

'What?' His voice was huskier than normal. He cleared his throat.

'When you're deprived of one sense, your others are heightened,' she whispered, low and throaty, almost challenging, and so close to his partially covered ear that he felt the warmth of her breath.

'Stop teasing the boy,' Mimi said.

'What?' Caroline said, as she moved away. 'I'm just saying he has a better chance of identifying the real apple pie with his eyes covered.'

She served Travis's plate last. He used the opportunity of her closeness to pull her on to his lap.

'Aah!'

'Oh no you don't.' He held her in place despite her immediate attempt to wriggle free. 'Since you were so thrilled to blindfold me, you can be the one to feed me.'

She stilled, and he loosened his hold, leaving his left hand resting on her hip.

He passed the taste test, easily identifying the real apple pie. Karl failed on his second attempt, to everyone's amusement.

'What led you to New Mexico?' Mimi asked him.

Caroline held her coffee cup with two hands and leaned back into Travis's shoulder, evoking comfortable memories.

'I was able to trace Grossvater from his recruitment to Rommel's Afrikakorps. Then the records become confusing. According to at least one account, the soldiers' German papers were confiscated by their captors and not returned. Some weeks later, new prisoner identification papers were issued. But none in Grossvater's name. He seems to have disappeared.'

'But what about the letters?' Lou asked.

'I read somewhere that it was not uncommon for prisoners to give an alias, a number of them going so far as to destroy their own papers,' Travis said.

'I suppose. He signed all his letters simply *your loving husband*, no given name.'

'So you hit a dead end, no pun intended,' Lou said.

'I had basically decided that I would never know, but I had several sophisticated search engines combing the internet. And it came back with the website posting of your discovery.'

'You had it searching for mummies?' Caroline asked.

'It picked up the comments on a Nazi in New Mexico, two of my parameter words.'

'Because one of the pouches had a swastika-like design, people assumed the mummy was a Nazi?' Mimi said.

'Some,' Karl said.

'You did,' Travis said. He felt Caroline lean forward and he hugged her closer. Now was not the time to reveal the secret of the eagle that only the two of them knew. In his peripheral vision he saw her bite her bottom lip and knew she understood. He patted her thigh to let her know he appreciated her effort.

'Yes, but that isn't the only reason I came here,' Karl said. 'I must have read his letters a dozen times before I finally started picking up clues. He wrote about finding a piece of strange quartz while weeding in a field of onions. One of the other prisoners told him the spider veins through the glass-like substance were made of gold. He wrote of the fascinating legends of the area. He was sure he'd solved the secret of the lost Vanderveer fortune. Every letter after that had some mention of becoming wealthy.'

'He was bitten by the treasure-hunting bug,' Mimi said.

'Because he thought he was smarter than the locals,' Travis said. 'I read the letters, too, after you gave them to me, and was struck by his inflated ego. He wouldn't get his loose

147

teeth treated because he was sure the camp dentist was an escaped German Jew. He felt demeaned by labouring in the fields alongside ethnic workers and only did it because it was the one source of income offered to a POW. He raged about the camp conditions even as he admitted that his counterpart in Germany probably wasn't getting three square meals a day, medical treatment and a clean bed.'

'I agree. He was a man of his time. I try not to judge him based on my beliefs.'

'That's mighty wishy-washy, Lou said. 'Can't you just say he was wrong?'

The pause was a heartbeat too long.

'Of course he was wrong,' Karl said.

'Dead wrong,' Travis added. He swung his legs to the side so Caroline could stand. 'I hate to be a party pooper, but it's getting late,' he said. 'We should be going. Lou may be a night owl but I need my beauty sleep.' He waited for Karl to take the hint and say good night. When he didn't, Travis asked him, 'Where are you staying?'

'Arbor Inn.' Karl finally got the message and stood. 'I should be going too. Thank you for a delightful evening,' he said to Mimi with a formal bow. 'I greatly enjoyed my visit in your lovely home.'

'I'll get my keys,' Caroline said.

'Wait.' Travis reached out and touched her

arm. 'My car is parked behind yours. Since I have to move it, why don't I take Karl back to the Inn? You can see Lou home.'

'No need for any of you to go out of your way,' Karl said. 'I'll call a taxi.'

'We only have one cab in Haven, and Melvin doesn't drive after dark,' Mimi said. 'His eyes, you know.'

'I'll drive Karl to the inn,' Travis said to Caroline, his expression defying her to challenge him.

'Fine with me,' Caroline said, raising her hands to signal her acquiescence.

As he backed out of the driveway, Caroline came running down the front stairs of the house. He stopped and rolled down the window.

'I thought of this just after you left,' she said to Karl. 'One of my clients is a former POW who stayed in the area after the war. Maybe he remembers your father.' She passed him a card on which she'd written Jurgen Petersen's name and phone number. 'Why don't you give him a call?'

'Thank you. I will.'

She stepped back and waved goodbye.

Travis looked in the rear-view mirror and saw her put her cell phone to her ear. He couldn't help wondering who would call her this late at night.

8

'The baby's coming.'

'What?'

'Which word didn't you understand?'

Caroline blinked and shook her head as she turned and ran for the house. The voice belonged to Dee Ann but Caroline had never heard her sound so like Linda Blair in *The Exorcist*. 'Stay calm.'

'Easy for you to say. This baby is coming early and Stephen is still in Santa Fe.'

Caroline's first reaction was to hang up and call Travis. Instead she asked, 'Did you call 911?' as she entered the kitchen.

'What's wrong?' Mimi asked, jumping to her feet and placing her hand over her heart. 'Who are you talking to?'

Caroline covered the receiver. 'It's Dee Ann. The baby's coming,' she said. 'And Stephen is four hours away.'

'Tell me something I don't know,' Dee Ann said, as cranky as before.

'Now listen carefully,' Caroline said to her sister. 'I want you to hang up and dial 911. Or I can make the call for you.'

'No, I can't go to the hospital in an

150

ambulance and leave Julie here alone.'

'Keep her talking and time her contractions,' Mimi said, 'I'll be right back.'

Time her contractions? How was she supposed to do that?

'I thought Julie was staying over at Savannah's.' Caroline didn't hear any response except strange heavy breathing. 'Dee Ann?'

'Whoo, whoo, whoo. She changed her mind and came home because she was worried about me.'

Mimi tapped Caroline on the shoulder. She had the strap of a canvas bag over her arm. 'I'm ready. Let's go.'

'Okay, we're on our way.'

'Tell her not to push,' Lou said as she climbed into the back seat.

'You tell her.' Caroline handed the phone to Mimi so she could concentrate on driving. Why was there so much traffic?

'Everything is going to be fine. Is Julie awake? Good. Tell her to get dressed and to pack an overnight bag. Okay. Yes, I understand. Now, I want you to hang up and talk to Julie while she does her errands. She'll be calm as long as you remain calm. We'll be there in a few minutes.' Mimi flipped the phone shut. 'Can you drive any faster?'

The calmness in her voice worried Caroline all the more.

151

'Call Travis,' she said over her shoulder to Lou. 'Tell him to meet us at Dee Ann's house.'

★ ★ ★

Travis beat them there because the Arbor Inn was just a few miles further down the road. When Caroline and the others arrived, he and Karl had interlocked their forearms into a fireman's carry and were transporting Dee Ann out to his squad car. Julie followed, carrying two small bags, which she dropped with a cry and ran to Mimi's arms.

'There's a blanket and some pillows on the sofa,' Travis said with a jerk of his head towards the house. 'We can use them to cushion Dee Ann's ride.'

'I hope nobody's puked in that back seat recently,' Lou said. 'Squad cars can be filthy.'

'I can drive her in my car,' Caroline said.

'Just get the pillows.' When she hesitated, Travis added, 'You don't have a siren, and I cleaned my car this morning.'

Caroline ran to fetch the items and arranged the blanket on the back seat of the squad car. Dee Ann had a contraction as Travis helped her in. She grabbed a handful of his shirt and twisted it in her fist, pulling him halfway into the car with her. He calmly

152

coached her breathing through the contraction and afterwards she managed a thank you and a weak smile.

'You're doing great,' Travis said. 'We'll have you to the hospital in no time.'

'I'm pre-registered at Providence Birthing Center in El Paso.'

'We're not going to make it that far. Your contractions are less than four minutes apart. Rather than have your baby born somewhere on the side of the highway, I strongly suggest you let me take you to the hospital. Okay?'

After a moment's hesitation, Dee Ann sniffed and agreed.

Travis backed out of the seat and Caroline handed him the pillows. He tossed one to Karl on the other side of the car to put under Dee Ann's head. The other two he tucked under her knees.

'How do you know to do that?' Caroline asked. 'Helping her with that breathing stuff?'

'Part of my emergency training. Cops have been known to deliver babies, you know.'

A minute later he was ready to leave.

'Caroline?' Dee Ann called.

Travis rolled down the automatic window.

'I'm here. We'll follow Travis to the hospital.'

'No! I want you to take Julie to Mimi's so I don't have to worry about her.'

'Sure, but don't you want Mimi to come to the hospital with you?'

'Julie first. You come after making sure she's settled. Okay?'

'Sure,' Caroline said. Even though it wouldn't have been her choice, this moment was all about what Dee Ann wanted. Only after Travis took off with lights flashing and siren wailing did Caroline notice that the suitcases were still on the lawn where Julie had dropped them. One of those should have gone with Dee Ann.

She got everyone in the car, Mimi, Julie and Lou in the back seat, and Karl in the front passenger seat. Rather than doubling back to drop him at the Inn first, she decided he could ride to Mimi's and then she could stop on the way to the hospital to let him off.

* * *

By the time she pulled into a parking place at the hospital, she felt as if she'd been driving for hours instead of just forty-five minutes. She paused to give Stephen a call, since she would have to turn off her phone inside the hospital. She wanted to be able to tell Dee Ann not only that he was on his way but also approximately where he was. She told him Dee Ann was at the hospital and that so far

154

everything was fine.

'How can that be?' she asked when he said he was less than an hour away. 'Are you driving a hundred miles an hour?'

'Ninety-five.'

'And you're talking on the phone? Are you crazy?'

'I'm not driving. Travis called a friend of his to give me a ride.'

'Okay, but you still need to slow down. You won't be doing Dee Ann any favours by showing up here on a stretcher.'

'We'll drive the speed limit. I promise.'

'In that case, I'll tell Dee Ann you're about an hour and a half away. And I'll call you back in fifteen minutes with an update.'

Locating Dee Ann took almost that long. Since most women delivered their babies in El Paso, tiny Haven Hospital had closed its maternity ward. Even though the parking lot was full, there was no one was behind the information desk at the main entrance to tell her where to find her sister. One nurse she corralled thought they would have taken Dee Ann to the Emergency Room, but that area was swamped with the debris from a sizeable bar fight. Another harried nurse suggested the surgery, but they too were full and backed up. Finally, with the help of the janitor, she found her sister in a corner of the closed cafeteria.

A hospital bed had been placed behind folding screens made of metal frames holding fabric curtains. Caroline approached with trepidation. She could hear Dee Ann panting and the low murmur of Travis's voice encouraging her. She waited until her sister blew out a long breath and he said, 'Good job,' before she came around the screen.

'Hi. I talked to Stephen and he's on his way.'

'Here,' Travis said, standing and stepping back as he drew her forward to Dee Ann's side. 'You can take over for — '

'No, I can't. I don't know how.'

'Don't leave me,' Dee Ann said.

'Don't leave her,' Caroline echoed.

'I'm just going to check with the doctor. You'll be fine, and I'll be right back.' He turned to Caroline. 'Wipe her brow with a cool cloth and give her some ice chips. You'll be okay.'

After Travis left, Dee Ann said, 'Do I look as bad as I feel?'

'Not at all,' Caroline lied. She sat on the stool Travis had vacated. 'Stephen is about an hour away.'

'I hope he's not driving like a bat out of hell.'

'I made him promise to stick to the speed . . . Oh dear. What am I supposed to do?' She hollered for Travis. 'Uh, breathe?' Caroline would have backed away, but Dee Ann had grabbed her hand and was squeezing it. Hard.

Travis came running. He sidled in next to Caroline.

'Focus, Dee Ann,' he demanded, and she blinked her eyes open to look at him. 'Now pant, one, two, three, and blow. Again, one, two, three, and blow. Can you feel the contraction ending? Good. Relax. Deep cleansing breath. Good job.'

'Where is the doctor?' Caroline asked.

'On his way,' Travis said. 'Providence Hospital in El Paso is sending a trauma team to transport some of the bar-fight rubble that was brought into the Emergency Room. Dee Ann's doctor hitched a ride with them. They should be landing in a matter of minutes.'

'Do you need to be in the ER arresting someone?' Dee Ann asked, trepidation in her voice.

'This case belongs to the state police. The biker bar where the fight took place is way out on Highway Fifty-four, miles outside my jurisdiction.'

Dee Ann dropped her head back on the pillow. 'I'm glad.'

A small dark man with a neat moustache wearing thick glasses and a bright red bow tie came around the screen. His entourage of three nurses served to enhance his air of importance. He paused and looked Travis up and down. 'You are not the father, no?'

'Oh, Dr Galeno, you're here,' Dee Ann said. From her voice, she was about to cry with happiness. Or maybe it was relief.

'Yes, little mother, I am here. Soon we have your baby, yes?' The doctor looked around. 'This is certainly not ideal but we must make do.' He turned to Travis. 'Get out.' His shooing motion included Caroline. 'Both of you. I must examine her.'

The two refugees sat at one of the nearby Formica-topped tables and waited.

A nurse came out of the sequestered area and ran from the room. She returned a few minutes later with a cart of equipment, most of it either wrapped in or under green cloth.

Caroline found Travis's hand.

A different nurse ran out and returned with a mobile incubator.

Caroline bit her bottom lip. Travis covered her hand with his free one.

'Is all this normal?' she whispered.

'I guess so.' He quirked his lips in a half-smile. 'This is the first time I've seen a baby being delivered in a hospital cafeteria.'

'You did a great job with Dee Ann earlier.' Caroline couldn't help but think that he would be a good coach when he became a father himself. And he would make a good father, too. He deserved the chance to have a family.

The third nurse came out from behind the screen. 'Is the father here?'

Caroline jumped up. 'Omigod. I totally forgot to call Stephen again.'

'I called him when I went out to check on the doctor,' Travis said. 'He'll be here in fifteen or twenty minutes,' he said to the nurse, who nodded and disappeared behind the curtain.

'Or sooner,' Stephen said as he walked across the room. He laid a helmet and gloves on the table. 'Is she in there?'

'Yes, and anxious to see you,' Travis said as he stood.

Stephen paused at the corner of the screen and turned to say, 'Thanks for the hook-up with Jimmy J,' before he called his wife's name and ducked behind the curtain.

Travis turned to greet the man who had followed Stephen into the cafeteria. 'JJ!'

'Travis, long time no see.' He barely glanced at Caroline. 'How you doing?' They did the mutual backslapping macho version of a hug.

'Thanks for helping out my friend.'

'What are pals for?'

'You made good time. What do you have? A little nitrous oxide tank hooked up to the fuel pump? A couple of JATO rockets under the hood?'

'Nah. Just my same old moonshine-guzzler Lucille. Okay, I did add a small throttle-in-a-bottle kit for kicks and giggles, but I don't use it often. Too hard on her motor.'

'Always respect the engine.'

Jimmy J leaned forward. 'I did get the old girl up to one thirty-seven on that straight stretch of new asphalt on Route Seventy.'

Caroline realized her jaw was hanging open and managed to shut it even though she was still too stunned to speak.

'Don't tell me anything I'll have to give you a ticket for,' Travis said with a grin.

'You'd have to catch me first. I'm looking at a six-fifty-horsepower Honeywell LT-101 turbine engine for my 'Vette. With a few modifications, that one might actually take to the air,' Jimmy J added with a chuckle.

'Better get a pilot's licence.'

'I'll keep that in mind. Well, gotta scoot. Catch you on the flip-flop.' With a thumbs-up and a broad wink, he left.

'Was that Jimmy J the race-car driver?'

'Of course.'

'I had no idea you knew him. He's fabulous.'

'You don't remember meeting him?'

'Believe me, I would remember if I ever met Jimmy J.'

'JJ is one of the local guys that used to hang out at the motorcycle races. You met him several times.'

'Oh.' The JJ she recalled had been skinny as a pencil and needed to see a dermatologist. 'I guess he didn't recognize me either.'

Travis ducked his head and nonchalantly traced the wavy pattern of the Formica-topped table with his finger.

When he didn't say anything, she realized the truth. Jimmy J had recognized her and purposefully had not spoken to her. She'd been snubbed. Given a cold shoulder that could freeze all the pole beans in hell. 'Oh, now I understand.'

'Don't hold it against JJ. He and Fortis were there the night your process server finally caught up with me to deliver the divorce papers. I don't remember much of the next three days, but I'm fortunate to have friends that stuck with me. When I sobered up, we were in Vegas. I had skinned knuckles, a broken nose, a real beauty of a black eye, and I was down three thousand bucks.'

'Doesn't sound like they took very good care of you.'

'Believe me, they did. It could have been

much worse. I wasn't in jail and I still had my wheels.'

Stephen stuck his head out and said in a thrilled voice, 'It's a girl.'

'Congratulations,' Travis called. Stephen had already gone back behind the screen.

Caroline sprang to her feet and grabbed Travis in an excited jump-up-and-down hug. 'It's a girl.' Then she suddenly remembered who she was embracing and she broke contact and stepped back. Unable to think of anything clever to say, she spun on her heel and headed for the curtained-off area.

She had barely entered the makeshift birthing room before she was unceremoniously shooed out by one of the nurses, who said, 'What are you doing? Doctor didn't say you can come in. Out. Out.'

Feeling a bit deflated, Caroline reurned to her seat at the table.

'Shouldn't you call Mimi? Your sister Mary Lynn? Your brothers?'

'I . . . I think I'll wait until I know a weight and length, because they're sure to ask. Besides that, Stephen and Dee Ann might want to make those calls together.'

'I'm glad he got here in time,' Travis said after a moment of awkward silence.

'Yes. He didn't appear to be disappointed that it's not a boy, either.' After two girls, Dee

Ann had been worried.

'Not all men are stuck on having a son. Stephen knows he's a lucky man.'

A flash of something in Travis's expression surprised Caroline. Jealousy? Longing? She'd never seen anything like it previously, but the look was gone before she got a good read. 'You'd be a great dad. Why didn't you ever get married again and have kids?'

'Why didn't you?'

'I asked you first.'

Travis sat back in his chair. 'I got close. A couple of times.'

So much for her thinking he'd been pining away for her all those years. Of course she hadn't really thought that. Although she had to admit she'd enjoyed a secret little thrill every time she'd learned from Mimi or one of her sisters that he'd separated from yet another girlfriend. 'Was one the tall, drop-dead-gorgeous blonde with the yellow sports car?'

He raised an eyebrow.

'Mary Lynn told me about her.' Although she would never admit it, there were times when having a tattletale little sister came in handy.

'Gretchen Rodriguez. She's a nurse at the Truth or Consequence Municipal Hospital. My first girlfriend . . . after you. And I came real close to asking her to . . . '

'Does she know you're back in Haven?'

'I had dinner at her house last week. She's a fabulous cook. Still makes the best stacked enchiladas in the state.'

'Oh.' Caroline's turn to trace the wavy pattern on the Formica.

'Her husband and twin boys love her cooking, too.'

'You had dinner with an ex-girlfriend and her family? Wasn't that awkward?'

'Why should it be? We're friends. The boys call me Uncle Travis. I'm friends with all my ex-girlfriends; well, most of them.'

'Me being the exception?'

'No. I always thought of you as an ex-wife. Different category.'

'So who's in the non-friend category? The stalker wench who had a thing for Chicago cops?'

'You know an awful lot for someone who was never around.'

'I came back to see the family at least once or twice a year.' At his raised eyebrow she added, 'Lou let the whole restraining-order thing slip that Christmas after a little too much eggnog.'

'My captain's idea. He thought she was a psycho and would shoot me with my own weapon.'

'Okay, so I understand why you didn't marry *her*, but why not Gretchen or any of the others?'

Travis grinned and shook his head. 'You make it sound like I dated hundreds of women.'

'I didn't keep count.'

'Neither did I.'

'You're avoiding the question.' Caroline leaned back and crossed her arms.

After long minute of silence he said, 'When I decided to be a cop, I knew I was choosing a dangerous profession. I never wanted to leave a wife and possibly a child alone.'

Caroline hesitated. Should she say something? They'd never talked much about his father's death. She'd only been six years old at the time and remembered very little. She did know he'd been killed while on duty. For Travis's sake she wouldn't let the issue slide. 'Like your father?' she asked softly.

'Not exactly a great leap of logic there.'

She took his hand in both of hers. 'Your mother understood the possibility when she married him, when they had a child.'

'This is Haven. No one expected bank robbers from El Paso to roar through town, or for them to shoot the deputy who chased them.'

'How do the friends and families of police

165

officers everywhere else deal with them going into life-threatening situations over and over?'

'I'm not sure how to answer that. Large departments in big cities have counsellors on staff to help loved ones cope. Here in Haven, I guess they just talk to Lou or Phyllis.'

'Good to know,' Caroline said. 'Since Bobby Lee is on the force and all,' she added quickly.

'Sure. I knew that's why you were asking.'

'And just for the record, people die every day. My father died in a plane crash. Does that mean I have to choose between flying and marriage?' Actually she was a nervous flyer and avoided it as much as possible, but that wasn't the point. 'Your mother was killed in a car accident. Does that mean everyone should avoid driving if they have children?'

'It's not that simple.'

'Maybe it is if you let it be.'

Travis opened his mouth but shut it without speaking when one of the nurses opened the screen.

'Meet your newest niece, Emma Louise Carson,' Stephen said as he carried the tiny bundle wrapped in a blanket towards Caroline. 'Eighteen inches tall and weighing in at six pounds three ounces.'

A nurse adjusted the pillow under Dee Ann's head while another one tucked in the fresh sheets. Behind Stephen the doctor cleared his throat.

'They're moving us to a room in a minute,' the new father said. 'And unfortunately visiting hours are already over. 'Do you want to hold her?' he asked Caroline.

She shook her head, but he didn't appear to notice.

'Meet your Aunt Caroline,' Stephen said, handing her over.

She had no choice but to take the infant. Of course, she'd held babies before, but not often, and never a newborn. The baby was so beautiful. Looking into her eyes was like looking into the wisdom of infinity. Emma stared at her new aunt as if she could see into her soul. 'She takes my breath away.'

'I'm ready to have her back,' Dee Ann said.

While Stephen and Travis shook hands and thumped each other on the shoulder, Caroline slowly walked to the bed. As much as she had not wanted to hold Emma, she now hated the thought of letting her go. She placed the baby in her mother's arms. 'You did good, sis. She's amazing.'

Dee Ann smiled her thanks. 'I think so too. Oh, I have a favour to ask. The last time I talked to Julie, she said to send her a picture so she could see it first thing in the morning. Would you send one to Crystal, too?'

'Sure.' Caroline quickly took a dozen photos on her phone before the nurses flipped up the side rails and started moving the bed. 'I'll come to see you tomorrow, and I'll bring Mimi and Julie.' She walked beside her sister. Stephen made calls and sent texts as he walked on the other side of the bed. Travis trailed behind, chatting in a low voice with the doctor about his return to El Paso.

'Bring Mimi in the morning, but make sure Julie goes to school. They have placement testing this week and she needs to be there. She can come afterwards,' Dee Ann said.

'She's not going to like that,' said Caroline.

'If you help her put the *It's a girl* stickers on the little boxes of M and Ms, she can take them to school and pass them out. I've already cleared it with her teacher.'

After going through two sets of doors and several hallways, one of the nurses halted Caroline and Travis at the third doors by saying, 'I'm sorry. You can't go beyond this point. Visiting hours are over.'

Caroline said her goodbyes until tomorrow. As the new parents, with sweet baby and entourage, continued on through the doors, Caroline blinked tears from her eyes. Travis put his arm around her shoulders. They stood in silence for several minutes, as if neither trusted themselves to speak.

Travis was the first to move by turning his back on the door. Caroline followed his lead and they walked slowly back in the direction they'd come.

'You didn't say why *you* never married again,' Travis said.

Caroline shook her head. She couldn't tell him that he'd been the yardstick against which all other men had come up short.

'Didn't you want children?' he asked. 'Or should I say, don't you want children?'

She smiled at the memory of holding little Emma that was still fresh in her heart. But then the ticking of her biological clock started resonating through her body like she was standing next to a thumping bass speaker at a rock concert. She had to get away from him before she said or did something she'd regret.

'Uh, I gotta go,' she said, back-stepping towards the nearest exit. 'Thanks for all your help. I'll, uh, see you . . . around . . . later.' She turned and walked away as fast as she could.

When the revolving door gave her a chance to look back without being obvious, Travis was standing right where she'd left him, a confused look on his face.

9

Caroline yawned and stretched as best she could while sitting at her desk. The combination of the late night at the hospital and the early morning putting stickers on candy boxes with Julie had taken its toll. Mimi had decided to spend the morning at the hospital, since Caroline needed to get to the office. She had to finish the article about south-western honeymoon hotspots she was writing for a travel magazine. Nine fifteen in the morning and she was ready for a nap. What a time to run out of coffee.

She considered walking over to the café for a cup of Jackpot Java, so named by Maybelle's late-night-poker-playing father, and guaranteed to keep you wide awake for at least three hours. But she was waiting for a call from the bandleader confirming the date for the Petersen event, and she had a few questions to ask him.

Her eyelids felt like sandpaper. Did she really want yet another reminder that she wasn't as young as she used to be? She went into the stock room and pulled out the emergency bag, the large canvas duffel she'd used over the years to carry all the things she needed at weddings. She'd started carrying first-aid supplies in a red zippered pouch and it had grown from there. So much so that she'd been forced to organize it for easier access.

She pulled out an old silver clutch purse that held sewing supplies and a key ring of safety pins. Then a nail polish repair kit with seven assorted shades of polish. In with the polish were two bottles of white correction fluid; a typist's best friend, it also covered dings to any number of things white. Like scuffed shoes or a scratched headpiece.

Another bag held rolls of tape; transparent, double-sided and even duct tape. Another had essentials like talcum powder, deodorant spray, hand sanitizer and lotion. A small white tackle box she'd found in a hardware store in Hawaii contained scissors of several sizes, a screwdriver set, a small hammer and a box of assorted nails and screws. Yes, she had used them to fix a bride's broken heel. More than once.

Halfway through the duffel, she found the giant plastic bag of make-up. She'd made a science of collecting samples and could supply a forgetful bride with twelve shades of lipstick, three different mascaras, four blushers, the ever-popular concealer, eyeliner in brown and black, eyeshadow in eight colours, and seventeen different fragrances. All in miniature or single-use sizes.

Next to the eyelash curler, brushes and applicators she found what she'd been looking for. Soothing eyedrops and her favourite cucumber gel eye pads. She swivelled her chair to the side, propped her feet up on the opened lower desk drawer and leaned back as far as she could. After applying the drops, she placed the disposable pads over her eyes with a relieved sigh. Five minutes. She just needed five minutes and she would be a new woman.

When the tinkle of the bell over the door woke her almost a full hour later, her feet slipped off the drawer, jerking her forward. She was groggy and a bit disoriented after being ripped out of her dream. Not one of her usual fantasies: dancing with Travis on a sunset-streaked deserted beach, kissing him by a pristine lake nestled among snow-covered mountains, making love with him in front of a cosy fireplace. She didn't recall the entire dream, but she woke up remembering holding a baby in her arms and Travis surrounding them both in the protective warmth of his embrace.

She blinked reality back into focus, and grabbed a tissue to dab at her eyes as she walked towards the door and greeted Enid with a smile.

'Are you too busy to see me?' Enid asked, tentative and almost apologetic.

'You have perfect timing,' Caroline said, directing Enid to a seat on one of the two sofas. 'I was just going to make some tea. Can I get you a cup too?'

'That would be lovely. I still have to shop for new drapes, pearl necklaces for the girls, and Suzanne's birthday is next week. Add to that my head is swimming from my computer class.'

Caroline returned carrying a tray with two cups, creamer, sugar bowl, and a plate of ginger cookies she'd taken out of the lunch Mimi had packed for her when she'd made one for Julie. Enid was looking through a spiral notebook.

'Here we are,' Caroline said.

Enid closed her notebook. 'Oh, thank you. I was just looking through everything the computer instructor covered about internet searches and security. She really stressed safety issues. She even showed us how to track what your kids are looking at. Of course, I don't need that, but I took notes so I can pass them on to my daughters.'

'That sounds like a good idea.'

'Oh, and I found these.' She opened a

manila folder and handed Caroline several pages of recipes, including Mock Scallops, Liberty Cake, and Mock Pistachio Ice Cream. 'I thought maybe you could give them to Lewis for his consideration. I don't want him to feel obligated to use them.'

'I'm sure he'll appreciate your contribution. And I have some contracts for you.' Caroline retrieved the folder from her desk. 'Take them home, read them and then either you or Jurgen sign both copies. Keep one and attach a deposit cheque in the designated amount to the other. When you're done, call me and I'll pick it up.'

Enid took the folder but didn't open it, just held it in both hands. 'I, ah, want to apologize again for Jurgen's behaviour.'

'Not necessary.'

'This mummy thing really has him upset.'

The bell over the door tinkled again. Both women looked up as Karl Volker backed into the room in order to pull a large bouquet of balloons after him. He turned around, his arms loaded with gift bags and a very large yellow teddy bear.

'I could use a hand,' he said.

Both women stood. Caroline rushed to help him. As she made a quick introduction, she noticed that Enid had suddenly become extremely pale. 'Are you all right?'

'I . . . I have to go,' Enid said in a rush as she gathered her things. She practically ran from the room.

Caroline stepped out the door after her. 'I'll see you at seven o'clock at Eugenia's,' she called.

No response, not even an acknowledgement that Enid had heard.

'That was kind of weird,' she said when she returned inside.

'I haven't had that sort of effect on a female since I was eight years old and I jumped in front of Ingrid Berek with a giant toad on my head.'

'Don't be silly. She probably got a severe case of indigestion or gas or something.' Caroline shook her head. 'Must be an older-generation thing. Mimi hates to even burp in public. Oh, rats, I didn't get a chance to tell her you wanted to meet her husband. Did you call him?'

'Not yet. I've been shopping.'

'Yes, I guess I can see that.'

'The bear and balloons are for the baby.'

'Emma Louise.'

'A girl. I always wanted a girl. And these two pink bags are for the big sisters, bracelets that say Big Sister. Not imaginative but I hope they like them. Ah, this is for Dee Ann. It's a medallion that can be a pin or a necklace with three pink roses in a circle. Appropriate? Yes?'

'That's lovely, but why the retail therapy?'

'The what?'

'Buying a bit of happiness? Shopping as therapy?'

'I miss my family. I hate being half a world away from them.'

'Understandable. When do you go home?'

'Four days. Although I'd like to see the matter to a close and take my grandfather home with me, I'm afraid it won't be settled in time. I must return to my business.'

'If you have to leave before it's settled, I promise to keep you informed.'

'Thank you.' He put his head down and his hand in his pocket. 'Oh, this is for you.' He pulled out a box and handed it to her. 'A small token of appreciation for helping me locate my grandfather.'

'We don't know that for sure.'

'I know. Go on, open it.'

Inside the box was a gold link bracelet with an adorable Egyptian mummy charm, an inch-long intricately enamelled sarcophagus. 'It's beautiful, but I can't accept this,' Caroline said.

'You must. I can't take it back, because it's engraved.

The date on which she'd found Poor Fred

was engraved on the bottom. The tiny sarcophagus opened to reveal a gold replica of a wrapped mummy.

'They didn't have a cowboy mummy,' he said. 'So this was next best. You can add more charms to the bracelet if you want.'

'This is so thoughtful. Thank you.' She gave him a kiss on the cheek and a big hug. 'I absolutely love my new bracelet.'

'Am I interrupting?' a deep voice asked from the doorway.

'Travis!' She stepped away from Karl.

'I can come back later,' Travis said, his tone sarcastic. Even though he made the offer, he stepped inside and removed his cowboy hat. 'When you're not so busy.'

'Now is fine. I don't have any coffee, but would you care for a cup of tea? Bottle of water?'

'No thank you. I came with some information about that matter we spoke of yesterday.'

'What matter?' she asked, distracted by putting on the bracelet.

'The confidential one.'

'Oh?' She frowned in confusion at first, but it soon dawned on her that he was referring to Ernest the eagle statue. 'Oh, *that* matter.'

She started towards the back of the office, saying to Karl, 'If you'll excuse . . . ' When

Travis didn't follow her, she retraced her steps and grabbed his arm. 'If you'll excuse us for a few minutes,' she said to Karl while pulling on Travis's arm.

'Don't go out of your way,' Karl said as he reached for the door. 'I really must be going. I have a . . . something to do. Goodbye.' He ducked out of the door.

'Thank you for the bracelet,' she called after him. Then she smacked Travis on his upper arm. 'What did you do to scare him away like that?'

'Me? I didn't do anything. I was standing here minding my own business. Can I help it if I was wondering why a relative stranger would be buying you jewellery?'

'If you scowled at him like you're scowling at me, it's no wonder he left shaking in his boots.'

'You seem to be holding up pretty good.'

'That's because I know you're a toasted marshmallow, all rough and crusty on the outside and ooey-gooey sweetness inside.'

'You're delusional.'

'Fine. Don't believe me, but I know what I know and you'll never convince me otherwise.'

'Just don't go spreading vicious rumours to that effect.'

She put her hands on her hips. 'Did you

say you wanted to talk about Ernest?'

'Who? Oh yes, the eagle statue. Yes. Well, I located the quote about *trapped in the land of his foes* from inside the drawer. It is from the epic poem *Iwein* by Hartmann von Aue. My reference places it from 1203 rather than Volker's guess of 1197.'

'Big difference.' She rolled her eyes.

'I deal in facts,' he said.

'So did the story provide any clues?'

'Iwein was a knight in King Arthur's court. To avenge a friend, he travels far away but is stopped in his quest by Ascalon, the keeper of the bridge. They battle. Iwein loses and is made a prisoner. A servant, Lunete, helps him to escape by giving him a magic ring. Eventually he marries the lady of the castle, Laudine.'

'I love a happy ending,' Caroline said with a contented sigh.

'Unfortunately, in the second part, Iwein wants to make a trip to his homeland to see his old friends. Laudine states that she will wait only one year for him. Iwein runs into another knight from Arthur's Court, Gawain, and they go on a series of adventures together. Iwein loses track of time and forgets his promise to Laudine. The servant Lunete finds him and takes back the magic ring. Iwein realizes he's lost his love and his lands, and he succumbs to madness. He strips off his armour and fine clothes and lives in the forest as a wild man.'

'Ugh. I feel sorry for Laudine.'

'Volker did say it was a story of star-crossed lovers.'

'Were you able to find out if there were any prisoners named Iwein?'

'Among the papers Volker provided was a list of all the prisoners' names. No Iwein. But since the carver also used the name Laudine, I think the reference was symbolic rather than actual.'

'So Poor Fred identified with Iwein, a prisoner of his enemies, and he thought of his lady as Laudine waiting for his return. Makes sense, but that doesn't help much in identifying him.'

'That's why I also checked the list for any prisoner with the initials E. W.'

'I didn't think about the letters after the date being initials. I guess I was so focused on the intriguing inscription. Did you find anyone with those initials?'

'Four.'

'So what do you do now?'

'Track them down. See which ones returned to Germany. With a little luck, only one remained here.'

'And he would be Poor Fred.'

'Most likely. However, there is a possibility he bought or was given the eagle. Or stole it, even. E. W. may simply be the artist's initials.'

Caroline shook her head. 'I don't think so.'

'Why?'

She shrugged. 'Intuition.'

'Right.'

'Are you discounting women's intuition?'

'There is no such thing.'

'This from a man who listens to his gut.'

'Come on, it's not the same thing. My gut feelings are based on subliminal memories of relevant experiences.'

'Keep telling yourself that, cowboy.'

He jammed his hat on his head. 'Right now my gut is telling me it's time to go. Before I say something I'll regret.'

'Guess what? My intuition agrees.'

He left. Caroline stomped to her desk and plopped down in her chair. The good news was that she no longer felt tired. Travis had revved her up more than two cups of espresso.

As she cleaned up the tray and cups from earlier, she noticed that Enid had left without the contracts folder. Caroline munched on a cookie and tried to concentrate on writing her article, but all afternoon she worried about the older woman. Several telephone calls only reached Jurgen's curt leave-your-message instructions. Finally, as she was closing the office for the day, she decided to take a drive out to the farm. She could deliver the contracts and check on Enid at the same time.

As she pulled up to the farmhouse, the housekeeper ran out the front door screaming, 'He's dead! Omigod, he's dead!'

10

Caroline slammed on her brakes. She got out of her car and ran towards the front door of the house. As she reached for her phone to call Travis, she hesitated, watching the housekeeper run done the path to the garden waving her arms and crying hysterically.

Bev Frye reached Enid, who carried a large basket full of vegetables as she stepped over and around plants on her way to the path. The older woman put her arm around Bev's shoulders. They talked for a minute and Bev appeared to calm down. Then they walked towards the house arm in arm.

'Is everything all right?' Caroline asked as they approached.

'Everything is fine,' Enid said. 'I didn't expect to see you until later at Eugenia's.'

'I . . . ah . . . brought out the contracts you forgot.' Caroline gestured toward Bev. 'Didn't you just scream — '

'She panicked when she found Jurgen sleeping on the sofa. He usually takes his siesta upstairs.'

'Oh no, Miss Enid. Mr Petersen is not

asleep.' Bev crossed herself. 'The smell of death . . . '

'That's enough, Bev. He probably ate too much sauerkraut last night.'

'Don't you want to at least check on him?' Caroline asked.

Enid set her basket down on the front stoop. 'He'll be very upset with me if I wake him. He takes his siesta every day from one thirty to four o'clock; his nap is sacred.'

'It's after five thirty,' Bev said.

Enid looked at her watch. 'Oh my, you're right. Jurgen must have overslept. The last few days he's hardly been to bed at all. Insomnia. If he finally got to sleep he'll probably be angry if I wake him.'

'You can blame it on me,' Caroline said. 'Tell him I've brought contracts for him to sign.' She handed Enid the folder.

'I'm not a good liar,' Enid said.

'It's not a total lie. I did bring contracts.'

'Please, Miss Enid, don't go in there. Just call — '

'Okay, I'll wake him. If only to prove to you that nothing is wrong.' Enid went into the house, closing the door behind her.

Bev folded her hands and closed her eyes, her lips moving in fervent prayer. Caroline wasn't sure what she should do. She'd delivered the contracts, so she had no reason to stick around except for being available to answer questions. That was a feeble excuse, but her intuition told her something was wrong. A shriek from inside the house validated her bad feeling.

'Somebody call nine-one-one,' Enid screamed.

Caroline dialled her phone even as she and Bev ran into the house. They found Enid standing by the sofa, twisting a handkerchief in her hands.

'I'm afraid Bev is right,' Enid said in a small, weak voice.

'Nine-one-one,' Caroline's phone said in a tinny voice. 'What is your emergency?'

'Phyllis?'

'Yes, this is Deputy Phyllis O'Connor.'

Her use of her rank was a subtle reminder that all emergency calls were taped.

'This is Caroline Tucker and I'm at the Petersen ranch. Jurgen Petersen appears to be dead.'

'Does he have a pulse?'

With a grimace Caroline placed a finger on the side of his neck. 'No pulse,' she said. 'His skin is a sort of dull grey colour and there is a distinct smell.'

'I've already dispatched the ambulance. It should be there in approximately fifteen to twenty-five minutes.'

'That long?'

'You are quite a distance from town.'

Caroline understood why the ranchers in the area were lobbying to raise taxes to support an emergency helicopter for the hospital. If Jurgen weren't already dead, he could have died from any number of conditions before receiving medical help.

'Do you want me to remain on the line?' Phyllis asked.

Caroline relayed the question to the other women, and when they shook their heads she said, 'That's not necessary.'

'Do you want me to call you when the ambulance is close?'

'That would be appreciated.' Caroline hung up. 'I guess there's nothing to do now but wait,' she said.

'In my day the body of the deceased was washed and prepared for burial by the family,' Enid said, her voice sounding sort of far away.

'Is that what you want to do?' Bev asked.

Enid shook her head.

'Can we talk somewhere else?' Caroline asked. 'In the kitchen maybe?'

'Good idea. I could use a cup of really strong tea,' Bev said. 'With a shot of brandy in it,' she added, muttering under her breath.

The women trailed to the kitchen, but Enid didn't stop there, instead going out the sliding glass doors to the patio. Caroline

186

followed, glad for the fresh, cool air. Enid settled at a table on the patio shaded by bushes that had been trained up and over a trellis roof. While they waited for Bev and the tea, Caroline tried to get Enid talking to bring her out of her stunned silence.

'Do you want to call your daughters?'

'Huh? Yes. No. What can I say? Heart attack?'

'If you call them, they could be here with you.'

'I don't want them to see him like this. I don't want them to remember this every time they walk into the house.'

'Is there a friend or other relative you can call?'

'I can't deal with anyone yet.'

'Okay.' Caroline stood. 'If you need anything . . . '

'No. Please.' Enid grabbed the younger woman's arm. 'Stay. Help me.'

'Your daughters . . . '

'She needs your calm logic, not their emotional hysterics,' Bev said as she set the tray of tea things on the table. She'd also brought several pads of paper, pens, and a list of emergency numbers from the kitchen phone.

When Enid took her mug with shaking hands, Caroline decided they should talk about something else for a few minutes. She looked around for a topic. Spotting the plants on the overhead trellis, she asked about the straggly clusters of pea-sized blue fruit.

'*Sambucus cerulea*,' Enid said: 'Indigenous to this area. Native Americans used all parts of the plant medicinally although I've never been sure how because the bark and leaves are poisonous. Also known as blue elderberries.'

'Like in elderberry wine?'

'Yes.'

'We made this year's first batch of wine last week — Jurgen and I have always been fond of it.' Bev said. 'We also make jam and dry the fruit in the dehydrator for use during the winter,' she added, encouraging the topic.

'In the old days, people believed that fairies and elves would appear if you sat under an elder bush on a midsummer night. I always wanted to try that,' Enid said, her voice drifting.

'The fragrance of the flowers is a mild sedative,' Bev explained. 'Those fairies and elves were probably the result of drugged dreams.'

'You're so practical,' Enid complained.

'And you usually are, too.'

Enid turned her head. 'Many Europeans believed the elder tree was inhabited by a spirit known as Elder Mother. The adage *tip your hat to the elder* referred to the tree, not to an older person.'

Bev checked her watch in an obvious manner.

Caroline nodded in agreement. 'Maybe we should talk about what needs to be done before the EMTs get here. You can set priorities.'

Enid shook her head.

'Once you have a plan, you can designate some tasks to each of your daughters. I'm sure they'll want to help you.'

The older woman put her empty cup on the tray and stood. 'I'm going to get you some of my elderflower infusion. It not only cleanses the skin, it will also fade those freckles.'

Caroline was tempted. None of the gazillion products she'd tried over the years had ever gotten rid of the bane of her existence. 'That's very sweet of you, but maybe some other time would be better.'

The doorbell rang. All three women jumped. Bev left to answer it.

'Ready or not, here they come,' Enid said.

Caroline wondered why she hadn't received a phone call saying the EMTs were near. Come to think of it, she hadn't heard a siren either.

'Should we go into the living room?' Enid asked.

Caroline didn't want to do that. 'I'm sure someone will come for you if they have any questions. We don't want to be in the way.'

'I don't mind admitting I'm relieved.'

Bev returned to the patio leading Travis.

'Please have a seat, Sheriff Beaumont,' Enid said.

'No thank you, ma'am,' he said. 'I wanted to personally let you know that I redirected the ambulance to another call. I decided on a purely non-medical basis that the injured boy had the greater need.'

'You did exactly the right thing,' Enid said.

'I checked your husband for signs of life on my way in.'

'And you found none.'

'I'm sorry for your loss. Representatives of the Rondale Funeral Home are outside if you would like them to handle transporting the body to town.'

'Yes, thank you.'

Travis returned to the front door and waved the others inside. While Marlene Rondale and her brother Joey negotiated the gurney up the front step and in the door, he moved a couple of chairs and the coffee table out of the way.

Beneath the table he found a ring, a thin, plain band. He looked at the dead man's hand, but his fingers showed no sign of him wearing a ring. He put it in an empty crystal dish on the table.

'I'll check him for time of death. Do you want anything else?' Marlene asked, shining her small bright flashlight at Jurgen's eyes and mouth.

'Sheesh, sis, why do you have to imagine every death is a probable homicide?' Joey asked. 'People die. It's natural.'

'Why do you have to act like every death is merely job security? You think this guy died of natural causes?'

'Yeah. He must be pushing ninety.'

'Bet you five bucks he was murdered.'

'Hah! You're on.'

Travis had been standing by, trying to ignore the arguing. Marlene Rondale was the only female in the family business with her five brothers. Her motto growing up was *never give an inch or they'll walk all over you.* Since she was also the County Coroner, Travis paid attention when she said *murder.*

'What have you got?' he asked her quietly.

'I won't know for sure until I can test the levels of carbon dioxide in his blood,' she said, opening the case of supplies for collecting evidence. 'But the bloodshot eyes and bruising around the nose and mouth are classic.'

'You're thinking asphyxiation?'

'Yep.'

'I don't see any sign of a struggle.' The old man was on his back, straight as a church aisle, hands crossed over his chest.

'He could have been laid out after death.'

'Or not.'

'Good point. I'll do a full tox screen. He might have been drugged, too.'

Using her strong flashlight and a pair of magnifying glasses, she examined the face. 'I've got some fibres.' Using long tweezers, she placed them in an envelope. Then she looked around and pointed to a pillow on a nearby chair. 'That one.'

Joey reached for the pillow and Travis slapped his hand away. 'Put gloves on before you touch anything,' he said. 'Have you got this?' he asked Marlene. They'd worked together before and he trusted her to process the crime scene to her usual high standards, and to keep her brother in line.

Travis met Caroline on his way to the kitchen.

'I'm just checking on progress.' She leaned sideways and looked around his arm. 'Why haven't they moved him yet?'

'Did you try to resuscitate him in any way? Give him chest compressions or artificial respiration?'

'Euew. No way. He was obviously dead.'

'Did you touch the body at all?'

'Phyllis told me to check his pulse.'

He wrote the information in his notebook.

'Why are you shaking your head like that?' she asked.

'Trace evidence may put you on a very short list of suspects.'

He stepped past her, but she followed him through the kitchen, talking the entire way.

'What do you mean, list of suspects? That means you think there's been foul play. Omigod. You think Jurgen was murdered. Who would have — '

'I don't know yet.' He paused and turned around. 'I'm going to question Enid Petersen now. I'd appreciate it if we aren't disturbed.'

'If you're asking me to guard the door, the answer is no way. In fact, I'm coming with you. Enid just lost her husband and she doesn't deserve to face an interrogation alone.'

'Jeez, it's not as if I intend to grill her under a hot light. I just want to ask her a few questions.'

'Because the wife is always the first suspect, right?'

'The *spouse* is a suspect because she *or he* usually has motivation, opportunity and access.'

Caroline reflected that if *she*'d been

married to Jurgen for all these years, his superior attitude would definitely have been motivation for murder. But then she wouldn't have put up with that sort of behaviour for as long as Enid had. As Lou had said, the woman must be a saint.

'Except in this case,' she said, 'the *spouse* is a sweet, gentle apple-dumpling of a woman who is older than your grandmother.'

'There have been more unlikely suspects who turned out to be guilty.'

'You can't really think she — '

'My job is to collect information and evidence, not judge guilt or innocence.'

Caroline ducked past him to the patio door. 'Just remember that,' she said over her shoulder. She took a seat next to Enid. 'Trav . . . Sheriff Beaumont wants to ask you a few questions.'

'Is something wrong?' She grabbed Caroline's hand. 'Will you stay with me?'

'Of course I will, but there's nothing to worry about. He's just collecting information. Isn't that right?' she said to Travis in a bright tone.

'Yes.' At Enid's nod, he took a seat across the table from the two women. He made a show of opening his notebook and writing the date and other pertinent data. 'What time did you find your husband?'

194

'Actually, my housekeeper, Bev Frye, found him when she returned from town around five thirty. She thought he might be dead and came out to the garden to tell me. I returned to the house and confirmed her suspicion. Then I asked Caroline to call nine-one-one.'

'What time did you get here?' he asked Caroline.

'About five thirty.' She sounded a little distracted even to herself, but she was wondering why Enid had sounded so matter-of-fact. Her rendition of the events had had none of the emotion she might have expected. 'Huh?' she asked when Travis cleared his throat.

'I asked why you are here.'

'Oh, I'm planning the Petersens' vow renewal ceremony. I delivered some contracts that need to be signed.'

'Did you have an appointment?'

'No.' What difference did that make, and why was Travis questioning her? 'I gave the contract folder to Enid this morning. She left it in my office, so I decided to bring it to her.'

When Enid visibly relaxed and reached for her tea, Caroline realized that Travis was simply putting her at ease.

'Why don't you tell me about your day,' he said to Enid.

'I . . . I don't know where to start.'

'Why did you go into town?'

'Computer class. I dropped Bev off at her daughter's house and was at the library when it opened at nine. After class I went to Caroline's office. We talked for a few minutes and then I came home.'

'What time did you get home?' he asked, his tone gentle.

'Maybe quarter to eleven.'

Travis scratched his head and looked through his notes as if he were confused. Caroline recognized yet another ruse to put the suspect at ease. He'd told her about this one. He called it *going Columbo*, after the TV detective, who was a master at making the suspect feel superior and thus lulling them into making a mistake.

'And your husband was home at that time? At quarter to eleven? Was he all right?'

'Fine. I fixed his usual Wednesday lunch of tomato soup and a grilled cheese sandwich and left it on a tray in the kitchen before I went out to the garden.'

'You should put some antibiotic on that scratch on your arm.'

Enid covered her arm with her other hand. After a millisecond of hesitation, she chuckled. 'My weakness for blackberries has cost me many such scratches over the years. I couldn't resist the last bowlful of the season. I

196

was hoping to make blackberry scones one more time and the recipe only calls for a half-cup.'

'So you were in the garden all afternoon. You do know that you should wear a hat and sunscreen.'

'Oh, I wouldn't think of going out without a hat.'

'What time did Bev return?'

'I can't say exactly because I tend to lose track of time when I'm taking care of my plants. I presume about the same time as usual, about one o'clock. When Jurgen takes his nap, we try to stay active outside the house so as not to disturb him.'

'Did she enter the house?'

'I didn't see her arrive. Probably not. Jurgen is . . . was a light sleeper.'

'And then?'

'Bev helped me in the garden for several hours before going inside to start dinner preparation. She couldn't have been in the house long before she found Jurgen on the sofa. She came running out to the garden at about five thirty.'

'Around the time Caroline drove up.'

'Yes, I guess so. I didn't actually see her arrive, but she was standing on the front porch when Bev and I came up the path.'

'Did anyone else come to visit? Anyone at

all? Friends, strangers, salesmen, delivery guy?'

'Not that I noticed.'

'Did Jurgen eat his lunch?'

'What?'

'I'm trying to ascertain a time of death, and I didn't notice any dishes as we passed through the kitchen, so I wondered if he ate his lunch. Did he usually clean up after himself?'

End gave a rueful chuckle and shook her head. 'Never. He might work like a dog doing outdoor chores on the farm, but once inside the house he never lifted a finger. As to your question, I didn't notice anything either. Maybe Bev cleaned up before she served tea.'

He nodded. 'Makes sense. Did you and Jurgen have any sort of disagreement earlier?'

Enid could not disguise the warm flush on her cheeks. 'He was so upset lately about the mummy being found on that strip of land he's been fighting with the government about for years. And then there was the additional tension of planning for the vow renewal. Except for getting to know Caroline, I wish he'd never come up with the idea.'

'His idea? Really? He didn't impress me as the romantic type.'

'He had his moments. But the vow renewal had a selfish motive. He'd been thinking about death more and more lately. He didn't want to meet his maker not having been married by a minister. Our wedding took place in the courthouse by a judge rushed between hearings.'

'Jurgen thought the two of you had been living in sin all these years?'

'In the eyes of some we had.'

'What do you think?'

'I think the vow you make in your heart is more important than who witnesses your public declaration.'

'Good answer,' Caroline said.

'So you argued about the vow renewal?' Travis asked.

'We argued about many things almost every day. I can't say today was any different.'

'Anything particular you argued about today?'

'Hmm.' Enid scrunched up her forehead. 'Drapes. I wanted new drapes before the event. Suzanne's birthday present. She's our youngest daughter and she wants a motor scooter. Jurgen thought it ridiculous for a middle-aged woman to ride around town on a scooter. But it's perfect for her because she only lives a mile from work. He wanted to get her a bicycle.'

Hardly motivation for murder, but he'd been surprised before at the things that made someone snap. 'Anything else?'

'Nothing particular, but maybe I'll remember something later.' She gave him a hopeful smile.

'Did Jurgen have a will? An insurance policy?'

'I'm sure he did. All of that would be with our lawyer, Walter DeShane. Junior now that his father's retired.'

'I'll check with him. Would you mind if I looked through Jurgen's office? Maybe take his computer for a few days?'

'Why? Aren't you supposed to have a warrant or something to do that?'

'Not if you consent. I hate to have to say this, but there are indications that Jurgen might not have died from natural causes.'

Enid put her hand to her throat. 'Are you sure? Murder?'

'We're still investigating. Your cooperation is appreciated and I promise to be as careful with his things as possible.'

'You can trust Travis,' Caroline said. 'He's the best at finding the truth.'

'Of course I'll cooperate. I just can't imagine who would do such a thing. I mean, Jurgen had plenty of arguments with farmhands and suppliers, but nothing that would justify murder.'

'Can you make a list of those people for me?'

'I can look up all the suppliers in the

200

business chequebook but I have no idea which ones he had disagreements with. Jurgen kept all his business notes on the computer in a file or something.'

'I can contact all of your suppliers.'

'As far as employees . . . '

'Current and former.'

'I'm sure there are tax forms of some sort in his office.'

Caroline leaned forward. 'He should have copies of W-2s.'

'That's what I was thinking of,' Enid said.

'I'll look for those after I talk to Bev Frye.'

'She's probably waiting in the kitchen,' Enid said.

As Travis rose, Marlene Rondale came out to the patio.

'We're ready to leave,' she said to him.

'I'll call you later for your results,' he replied.

She nodded and then turned to address Enid. She handed over a booklet. 'This will answer many of your questions. If you have any others, please don't hesitate to call. My card is inside the booklet.'

Travis excused himself to go talk to Bev. When Caroline started to follow him, Enid asked her to stay.

'When can we talk about the arrangements?' she asked Marlene.

201

'In my experience, it's not a good idea to make plans until the body is released by the County Coroner.'

'Isn't that you?'

'Yes, but I can't make any promises until after the autopsy, because I never know what I'm going to find. Best guess? Two days.'

'That long?'

'Maybe more.'

'It won't seem like a lot of time with so much to be done,' Caroline said gently. 'Starting with calling your daughters.' She looked at her watch. 'Which you'd better do quickly, before they all leave for Eugenia's Creations. You don't want them sitting there waiting for you.'

Enid pushed herself to a standing position. 'Thank you, Miss Rondale. I'll call tomorrow afternoon for an update.'

After goodbyes, Marlene left.

'I think I'd prefer to call the girls in private. If you'll excuse me, I'm going to use the phone in my bedroom. If you would please call Eugenia . . . '

'I can cancel the appointment without giving a reason.'

'Thank you. I won't keep you any longer. The girls will be here soon.'

'Please don't hesitate to call me if there's anything I can do.'

As Caroline was leaving the house, she held the door for Travis, who had his arms full with Jurgen's computer and a bag of papers and notebooks. They walked to their cars together.

'She's lying,' Caroline said, as soon as they were out of earshot. 'Hard to believe, but that sweet little old woman is lying through her teeth.'

11

As Caroline and Travis reached the parking area near the Petersens' house, he asked, 'Do you want to get a cup of coffee?'

'Are you asking me out on a date?'

Travis snorted in the back of his throat. 'If I ever ask you out, there won't be any doubt in your mind about my intent. I'm talking about stopping by the station.'

'Oooh, how enticing,' she said with a mock shiver of excitement.

He didn't even crack a smile. 'I'd like to ask you a few more questions.'

'Like why I think Enid is lying?'

'Not here,' he said in a lowered voice.

'Okay, I'll meet you at your office in an hour and a half. I want to see Dee Ann and Emma before it gets too late and I miss visiting hours.'

'I talked to Stephen before coming out here. They've released Dee Ann and the baby and they're at home.'

'What? It hasn't even been twenty-four hours.'

'I guess the good news is that they're doing so well.'

'Okay, I'll stop by their house.'

'Ah, the bad news is that Stephen's mother is in town for a couple of days.'

'Then again, maybe I'll let them get settled in tonight and stop by . . . later.'

Thereby avoiding Regina Carson. Not that she was a bad mother-in-law to Dee Ann, whom she liked, or at least pretended to like for Stephen's sake. And she absolutely adored her granddaughters.

But Regina had never forgiven Caroline for winning the holiday story-writing contest sponsored by the local newspaper. Regina had won the annual contest for so many years that few people even bothered to enter. Twenty-three years ago, Caroline had changed that. Her story about a Christmas rag doll that wanted to meet Santa won the one-hundred-dollar prize and praise as the best story they'd had submitted in ages.

She was eventually disqualified because she was only fifteen and the rules clearly stated that entrants must be at least eighteen years old. Regina was officially declared the winner, but by then her triumph had become a joke around town.

The next year the newspaper had changed the rules, making the contest for children only. Hugely popular that year and every Christmas after that. Not likely to change back. Ever.

No, Regina Carson did not like Caroline.

'So, I guess I'm free for coffee,' she said to Travis.

'I thought you might be,' he said with a crooked grin. 'I'll meet you there,' he added as he got into his car.

He backed out and waited for her to pull out. Then he followed her halfway back to town. When a semi zipped past them doing at least ninety, Travis turned his car around and gave chase with lights flashing and siren blaring.

With a bit of extra time Caroline decided to stop at Bubba Woo's Barbecue Pit and Sushi Bar for some takeout. She parked the car and called Mimi to let her know what had happened and that she wouldn't be home for dinner. As she walked towards the restaurant, she made a quick call to Phyllis to see if she wanted to order anything.

'Hi, Mrs Woo,' Caroline said to the woman behind the counter, so small she could barely reach the cash register.

'I'm fine as frog's hair.'

Caroline blinked until she figured out the woman must have thought she said 'How do you do.'

Mrs Woo grinned as if to show off her new movie-star-white dentures. 'What can I get you?'

Caroline looked up at the menu written on the wall. She of course would have her favourite, Bubba's dainty California rolls. He made them smaller than most so they were perfectly bite-sized rather than a huge mouthful. And she could eat twice as many. The question was what to get for Travis. Did he still have the same tastes as he'd had more than ten years ago? Did he even like sushi? She finally decided she couldn't go wrong with barbecue.

'Number four, a twelve, a small number seventeen, and a large twenty-two. To go.'

'Fifteen minutes. No problem.' Mrs Woo turned and hollered a stream of Chinese through a small window into the kitchen.

A few moments later, Bubba came through the swinging doors. 'Oba-san, come sit down. Let me wait on the customers.' He put an arm around the old woman's shoulders and led her to a rocking chair near a table with a tiny TV.

He returned with a sheepish smile. 'She loves to help out. Let me just verify your order. One barbecue octopus, one white-fish — '

'No, no. I ordered the pulled pork sandwich platter, dainty California rolls, a large order of fries, and a small miso soup.'

'I apologize.' He leaned towards her and

207

lowered his voice. 'Her hearing and memory aren't as sharp as they used to be.'

'I heard that,' the old woman said.

Bubba shook his head. 'She didn't really. She just says that whenever anyone lowers their voice. Your order will be ready in just a few minutes.'

While Caroline waited, she thought about her upcoming meeting with Travis to discuss Enid's lies. Maybe the older woman hadn't been lying. Maybe she just didn't remember as clearly as she thought she had. Enid hadn't appeared to be confused, but then neither had Mrs Woo.

★ ★ ★

Caroline arrived at the station in a thoughtful mood. She opted to stay out of Travis's private office and set up the fast-food picnic on the spare desk near the counter by the door. Bubba had included all the necessary accessories: napkins, plastic silverware, chopsticks, soy sauce, catsup, three steaming cups of green tea and fortune cookies. Phyllis was grateful for the soup and fries but she had to take them to her seat at the dispatch board.

Caroline waited for Travis and jumped up when the door opened.

'Don't I get a phone call?' a scruffy,

dishevelled stranger said as he entered. His voice was slurred and his eyes were watery.

Travis followed him in carrying Jurgen's computer.

Caroline lifted the section of counter top so the two men could enter the office area.

'Thanks,' Travis said. 'Sorry you had to wait.'

'No problem.'

He put the computer on Bobby Lee's desk and motioned his prisoner over. 'Sit down, Dwayne.'

'I want my phone call.'

'Your lawyer isn't going to do you any good until tomorrow morning,' Travis said, his voice firm but not unkind. 'You are going to sleep it off in one of the county's luxurious suites.

'Wasn't gonna call no stupid lawyer. I hate stupid lawyers.'

'Dwayne here just got his divorce papers,' Travis explained to Phyllis and Caroline. 'He's been . . . uh, celebrating.'

'I wanna call Doreen. Tell her I love her no matter what she did with those other guys.' Dwayne sniffled. 'I still love her,' he said to no one in particular.

Travis took off his handcuffs and handed him a box of tissues. 'Shut up, Dwayne. I told you in the car I've heard enough about

Doreen. Believe me, you're better off without her.'

Dwayne shook his head. 'You don't understand. Pretty women like her don't never pay no mind to good ol' boys like me. Doreen is so sweet when she wants something, just makes me want to buy her more stuff.'

'I'm here,' Bobby Lee announced in grand fashion as he entered the station. He ducked under the counter, and as he stood, he raised his hands, each holding a plastic bag from Charro's Grill. 'Please hold your applause until after dinner is served.'

'Dinner?' Caroline stepped in front of her picnic.

Bobby Lee put the bags on his desk. 'We have all the usual suspects, tacos and tamales and burritos. And the special of the day, green enchiladas.'

His thoughtfulness was unexpected. How did he know she was going to be at the station? Maybe Mimi had told him.

'That's very sweet of you.'

'Travis asked me to stop and . . . ' He sniffed the air like a bloodhound. 'I smell pork barbecue. Bubba Woo's.' He sniffed again. 'Fries and miso soup.'

'And California rolls,' Caroline said, stepping aside and making a motion worthy of a TV game-show hostess presenting the grand prize.

'I guess great minds think alike,' Travis said with a shrug.

'Cool,' Bobby Lee said, rubbing his hands together. 'Enough for me too.' He opened one of the bags, but turned to stone when Travis cleared his throat.

'I'm hungry,' Dwayne said.

'Deputy Tucker is going to process your paperwork,' Travis said to his prisoner. 'Then as soon as you're settled in your cell, he is going to take over dispatch so Deputy O'Connor can take her scheduled break. After that, she's going to give you lots of strong coffee and a back-to-Jesus talk like only a mother can.'

Dwayne twisted around in his chair. 'You're not going to call my mama, are you?' he asked Phyllis.

She looked to Travis for a decision.

He nodded for her to make the choice.

'Not if you behave yourself and listen respectfully,' she said. 'After that, I'll get you something to eat.'

'Thank you, ma'am,' he mumbled.

'Come on,' Bobby Lee said, taking Dwayne by the arm and helping him to stand. 'Your room is ready.'

'Hey, Sheriff, what about my truck?'

Dwayne asked over his shoulder, struggling against Bobby Lee's pull. 'You can't just leave it out there on the highway.'

'Deputy O'Connor will call the truck stop and have it towed to their yard.'

'What about my phone call?' Dwayne called as he and Bobby Lee disappeared behind a steel door.

'I sort of feel sorry for him,' Phyllis said, and Caroline nodded in agreement. 'He's not a bad kid.'

'Well, before you go all soft, he needs some straight talk,' Travis said, taking a seat across the desk from Caroline. 'He seems to respond to female authority figures, more so than men, so it's up to you to take the hard line with him.'

'Not surprising,' Phyllis said. 'He was raised by a single mother and he's got three older sisters. I'm quite sure none of them liked Doreen or thought she was any good. When he's ready, I'll introduce him to my cousin's niece, who's perfect for him.'

Except people don't always fall in love with the ones who are best suited to them. Caroline had tried. She'd dated guys like that. Take Walter DeShane, the county prosecutor. He was nice-looking, well-dressed and soft-spoken, polite and generous. They had interests in common, liked the same music, he wanted to settle down and have a family, and his idea of a great weekend was grilling steaks in the back yard and then watching a movie or having friends over. A perfect match for her.

But going out with him was like attending an art gallery opening with one of her brothers, if she could ever drag one of them to such an event, that was. No spark. No sizzle when body parts accidentally touched. No excitement, no heat. Not like when she was with Travis.

She jerked her head back and blinked at his hand waving in front of her face.

'Welcome back to earth,' he said with a grin. 'I asked you if you wanted to split this pulled pork sandwich with me.'

'Oh, no, you go ahead. I've got California rolls. And tamales,' she added so as not to reject his purchase. 'My favourites.'

'Together?'

She shrugged. 'Why not?'

'What were you thinking about?' He took a bite of his sandwich.

'Nothing. Why?'

'You had a strange look on your face.'

'What do you mean, strange? Like cross-eyed?'

'No, like . . . I don't know. I'm no good at this sort of description.'

She waited.

'Okay . . . maybe longing, or wistful.'

'Ha! That was simply hunger.' She popped a piece of her sushi into her mouth. 'Since I've been living at Mimi's, I've grown used to regular meals.'

'Grown being the operative word,' Bobby Lee said as he sat at his desk and opened the bag of tacos.

'Mind your own business,' Caroline said, conscious that she'd gained a pound or eight since returning to Haven. Yet one more reason she was anxious for her business to succeed, so she could move out on her own.

'Where's Dwayne?' Travis asked Bobby Lee.

He paused, his mouth wide open and an entire taco on its way inside. 'Um.' He put the taco down with obvious reluctance. 'Out like high fly ball to centrefield. As soon as I put him in the cell, he curled up on the bunk like a baby.'

'Did you take his belt?

Bobby was forced to pause again, put down his taco and answer. 'Yes, boss.'

'His shoelaces?'

'Yes, boss.'

'And anything else that he could use to harm himself?'

Bobby Lee's arm was going up and down

like a mechanical toy. Caroline stifled a giggle.

'Yes. This is not my first time processing a prisoner, you know.'

'Detainee.' When Travis turned to face Caroline, he gave her a broad wink. 'As far as I'm concerned, you make a few extra pounds look good.'

She wanted to change the subject, fast. 'I was thinking about what Enid said when you questioned her.' Talking about murder might not be the best dinner conversation, but it beat the heck out of the alternative.

'You mentioned as we were leaving that she lied. What makes you think that?'

'Maybe I shouldn't have called it lying. Maybe she just remembered incorrectly. After all, she is getting up there in years.'

'Did she show signs of a bad memory earlier?'

'No, I don't think so. Except there was one little thing. When I first met them, Jurgen said he'd told her to do something, and she hadn't, so that could have been a memory lapse.'

'So what made you think she lied?'

'Well, she said she always wore a hat in the garden, and yet I distinctly remember she didn't have one on when I arrived. And if she'd been in the garden all day like she said she was, wouldn't she have been at least a little bit sunburned? I mean, even the best sunscreen isn't that good.'

He grinned. 'I probably wouldn't have said it precisely like that, but I'm glad to have my observation seconded. Anything else?'

'Elderberry wine.'

'You mean like *Arsenic and Old Lace* high-school play elderberry wine?'

'Exactly what I thought of,' she said.

'Well, Enid makes her own elderberry wine, and Jurgen drinks some every day at lunch, you know, for his digestion.'

'And you're thinking maybe she mixed a teaspoon of arsenic, half a teaspoon of strychnine and a pinch of cyanide into a gallon of wine, just like in the play.'

'Not literally, but Bev did say the leaves and stems of the elderberry plant are poisonous. Whether or not they would knock someone out or just make them sick to their stomach, I don't know, but it's worth a second look.'

'I agree,' he said. 'I've already asked Marlene to do a tox screen, but I'll ask her to add testing for the chemicals found in elderberry bark and leaves.' Travis looked over his shoulder at Phyllis.

'I'm on it,' she said.

'Thank you.' He turned back to Caroline.

'Unfortunately, we won't get the results back from the state lab for a week at the soonest.'

Caroline popped the last dainty California roll in her mouth.

'What about the scratch on Enid's arm? I had the impression you wanted to say something when I noticed it but you held back.'

'It's probably meaningless, but I spent more than a few minutes looking at the basket she brought back from the garden while she went into the house alone.'

'And?'

'I don't remember there being any blackberries in it. To be fair, there could have been a container under the tomatoes or carrots, but berries are delicate and common sense would say to keep them on top of the other items.'

'You think she got the scratch some other way?'

'Yes. No. I don't know. We're talking like she's guilty, and I just can't see that sweet little old woman killing a fly, much less the man she was about to remarry in two weeks.'

'Hey, boss,' Bobby Lee called from his desk. 'You want me to hook up this computer?'

'I'd planned on contacting the state lab to send someone down to perform an analysis.'

'Let me see what I can do first. I learned quite a bit about computers from Bobby Ray.'

Caroline refrained from commenting on the dependability of lessons learned from someone currently on parole for robbery.

'Go ahead,' Travis said. 'But if someone comes down from state and says you screwed it up, you're on the hook.' He turned to Caroline. 'Those were some good clues you picked up on,' he said. 'If your wedding business is too slow, you can always open up a detective agency on the side.'

'And change the name of my business to Shackled?'

'Better than Celebrations. Too generic.'

'That was the point. I thought I'd have a greater chance of success if I took on other events, like the Petersens' vow renewal.'

'And the princess bride party?' Travis said with a sly grin.

'How did you hear about that?'

'We all heard about that,' Phyllis said, seconded by Bobby Lee.

'One of Harlan's daughters went to the party and couldn't talk of anything else for weeks,' Travis explained.

'And therefore Harlan had to tell us absolutely everything,' Bobby Lee said.

'Mostly he told us what his daughter wanted for her next birthday party that he couldn't afford on a deputy's salary,' Phyllis said. 'That boy's still bucking for your job, Sheriff.'

Travis shrugged. 'Tell him to get his name on the ballot.'

'He already has,' Bobby Lee said. 'His daddy agreed to be his campaign manager, and who should know more about getting elected than the mayor?'

'Is Lou going to be your campaign manager?' Caroline asked Travis.

'I don't have time to waste on glad-handing politics. If the town wants to vote Harlan into office, then he's what they deserve.'

'Are you worried?'

'Should I be?'

'Hey, guys, I got it working,' Bobby Lee said, patting the computer like a good child. 'I just hooked his CPU up to my peripherals and *voilà*, here's the history of his activity. Ah . . . anybody here speak German?'

'Not me,' Phyllis said. 'I took Spanish in high school. The German Air Force has a flying training centre at Holliman Air Force Base. We could get a translator from there.'

'I doubt they're open tonight. Make a note to call the public relations office tomorrow,' Travis said.

'But it makes sense,' Caroline said. 'German was his native language and he probably never even heard English until he became a POW. Omigod, I totally forgot Karl said he was going out to the Petersen ranch this morning. He was going to see if Jurgen remembered his grandfather. Do you suppose he saw anything?'

'Do you think he might be a suspect?' Travis said.

'But what motive would he have?'

'That would be one of the questions we want answered,' Travis said. He directed Bobby Lee to bring Karl Volker into the station.

The deputy jumped up. 'I'm on it, boss.' He started in one direction, then quickly changed to the other and stopped. 'Should we set up a roadblock on the highway?' He spoke fast and jerked his hand through his hair. 'Should I put out an APB? What kind of car? Does he even have a rental? I'll call the car rental company at the airport. And also all the agencies at the El Paso airport in case he — '

'Hold up just a minute,' Travis said with a chuckle. 'Your enthusiasm is commendable, but let's start with the simplest choice.'

'What would you do?' Bobby Lee asked.

'I'd call the Arbor Inn to see if he's in his room.'

'Done,' Phyllis said. 'According to Paula,

Volker checked out about an hour ago. He had her book a room for him at the Radisson airport hotel in El Paso, saying he had an early-morning flight.'

Caroline's phone beeped, signalling that she had a text message. It was from Bobby Ray, saying that Karl had been there to see Mimi. He was also looking for Caroline. Her brother wondered why. So did she. Mimi had told him where to find her.

'Call the Rad — ' Travis said.

'Done,' Phyllis responded. 'Volker arranged for a late check-in. They don't expect him before nine o'clock.'

'So where did Karl Volker go?' Caroline asked.

12

'Apparently Karl went to see Mimi,' Caroline said, sharing that part of her text message. 'He's probably coming here next.' She started to clean up the debris from the impromptu picnic she'd shared with Travis and his deputies.

'Why?' Bobby Lee asked.

She shrugged. 'To say goodbye?'

Travis helped her clean up and then handed the full trash bag to Bobby Lee. 'Check on Dwayne on your way back. If he's still sleeping, put these leftovers in the fridge for later.'

'Good evening, everyone,' Karl said, entering the station carrying two white boxes.

'Hi,' Caroline said, hiding her phone behind her back as if her forewarning text somehow made her guilty of something.

'Come on in,' Travis said, raising the counter so Karl could walk into the office area. 'We were just talking about you.'

'Ah . . . I sort of got that feeling. Why were you talking about me?'

'Why don't you have a seat? I have a few questions and then I'll explain.'

Karl sat slowly, his expression confused and anxious. 'What's going on?'

'Did you go to see Jurgen Petersen this morning?'

'Yes. Right after I left Caroline's office. Why?'

Travis pulled out his notebook. 'So that would have been about ten forty-five? You drove directly there?'

'Yes. Ah, no. I didn't want to show up empty-handed to ask him to spend time with me recalling his POW years. I stopped to pick up a gift basket, you know the sort with crackers, cheese, mustard.'

'Where was that? Do you have a receipt?'

Karl crossed his arms. 'Why are you asking me all these questions?'

There was a long moment of silence during which everyone looked at Travis.

'Jurgen Petersen was found dead earlier today. There were indications that foul play may have been involved.'

'And you think I — '

'I'm just gathering information. You may have seen someone or something that is relevant to the investigation.'

Karl pulled out his wallet and after a moment searching through a handful of receipts gave one to Travis. 'This is for the basket that I wound up giving to Mimi, because I never saw Herr Petersen.'

Travis raised an eyebrow.

'I drove out there, but no one answered the door. I walked around a bit. I only saw one man working near the barn and he didn't speak much English. When I asked for Herr Petersen he shook his head and indicated he didn't know his whereabouts. It was quite warm and I realized I should have phoned for an appointment. So I left. Went back to the Inn.'

'Did anyone see you return?'

'I expect so. It's not as if I was skulking about.'

'Please don't be offended,' Caroline said. 'I felt like I was getting the third degree myself, but I realized Travis is only trying to get all the facts.'

Karl jutted out his chin. 'What else do you want to know?'

'You're leaving?'

'Not that it has anything to do with your investigation, but yes, I decided to return home. I miss my boys more than I thought I would. Even though they're at school, two hours' drive is much closer than half a world away.'

'What about your search for your grandfather?' Caroline asked.

'I'm not giving up, but there's nothing else

to do here that I can't accomplish long distance. Perhaps when I have access to more evidence, I will come back. I'd like to bring my boys. I'm sure they would enjoy seeing the sights and meeting the people I'll tell them about when I relate my adventures.'

'They'll get a kick out of the giant pistachio, too,' Bobby Lee said.

'I'm sure they will.'

'I thought you needed to know where you came from to know yourself,' Travis said.

'Last night Mimi said that we are the sum of our decisions and that what we decide to do or not to do affects not only ourselves but also our children. Heritage is important, knowing where I came from is valuable, but not at the expense of time spent with my children. So I'm going home. My search is now relegated to the status of a hobby, not an obsession.'

'That sounds good,' Travis said. 'Except for one thing. You're a material witness in a possible murder case. I'm asking you not to leave town just yet.'

'Asking?'

'If you'd prefer I could arrest you or get a — '

'I am not a citizen of your country. What about diplomatic immunity?' Karl's accent got thicker as he became more upset.

'Are you travelling on a diplomatic passport, acting in a diplomat capacity, conducting diplomatic business?'

'You know I am not. I am here as a tourist.'

'Then there's no diplomatic immunity for you. Your choice is to go back to the Inn or join Dwayne in the cells.'

Karl shook his head and raised his eyes upward. 'This is like some huge cosmic joke. I was just talking about being the sum of our decisions because I'd made the decision to go home, and now you say I can't.'

'I'm sure it's just a delay of a day or two,' Caroline said.

Travis remained silent.

Did he believe Karl might be involved in the murder? But there was no motive. According to Karl, he'd never even met Jurgen.

'Of the two choices given me, I take returning to the Arbor Inn,' Karl said stiffly. He set one of the white boxes on the desk in front of Caroline. He started to give the other one to Travis, but paused mid-motion and turned to shove the box into Bobby Lee's hands. 'I found a German bakery in El Paso that made Wainachsrollen, a traditional almond cookie that Oma used to make for me. I meant it as a goodbye gift, but now it's a hello-again present.'

'Thank you,' Caroline said.

'Thanks,' Bobby Lee said, his mouth already full. 'These are mighty tasty.'

Karl nodded his head, almost a formal bow. 'I have some phone calls to make.' He paused, his hand on the door handle. 'Since I have to stay, I may as well tell you that when I was at the Petersens' door, I heard arguing coming from inside.'

'You didn't say that earlier.'

'You didn't ask if I'd heard anything, only if I'd seen anything.'

'That's splitting frog hairs.'

Karl shrugged. 'It could have been a radio or television. Since no one opened the door, I couldn't say for sure. I decided my presence would be *de trop* and I left.'

Dwayne wandered out from the cell area, stocking-footed, his hair standing out in all directions. He scratched his head with one hand and his belly with the other. 'I seem to have lost my truck.'

At Travis's direction, Phyllis guided him to a seat at Harlan's desk and Bobby Lee fetched food and hot strong coffee.

'Is there anything else that I should know?' Travis asked Karl.

'I've told you everything. And now I will say good night, if not goodbye.'

After Karl had left, Caroline stood and

227

said, 'I should be going too.'

'I'll walk you to your car,' Travis said.

'That's not nec — '

'I know, but I'll do it anyway.'

'Truly, I'm fine on my own.'

'I want to,' he said. 'I'd like a moment to talk to you, privately,' he added in a whisper.

'Oh.' She glanced around. Phyllis was bent over her switchboard, one hand over her headset as if to point out her covered ears. Bobby Lee stared at a cookie as if the secrets of the Sphinx were written there. Even Dwayne looked away, whistling under his breath as he stirred his coffee. 'Fine,' Caroline said. And just so everyone would know they wouldn't be discussing personal matters, she added, 'I have a few questions to ask you about the case too.'

He flipped up the counter section for her and opened the station door.

'Before you go,' Phyllis called, waving her hand in the air to get Travis's attention. 'I'll tell him,' she said into her mouthpiece before turning to face the others. 'Marlene wants to see you. Something about the numbers not adding up.'

'Thank you,' Travis said. He took Caroline's elbow and guided her through the door.

She followed his lead silently until they were outside the building. 'Isn't Poor Fred at

Rondale's? I could go with you and while you talk to Marlene I could find a way to slip the eagle into — '

'He's locked up.'

'I'll ask her to show me that he's safe and properly cared for.'

'Won't she take that as an insult?'

'I wouldn't think so. After all, I did find him and it's natural that I have an interest in his welfare.'

'Okay, I doubt you'll get a chance, but here's Little Ernest just in case.' He pulled the statue out of his pocket and gave it to her. 'We'll have to take separate cars. I'm still on duty.'

'I understand,' she said as he opened her door for her. 'I'll follow you to Rondale's.' While he jogged across the parking lot, she put the eagle in her purse. He drove to the exit and she pulled her car behind his.

The funeral home was only minutes away, because in a small town everything was only minutes away.

'Do you want the key to the elevator?' Joey Rondale asked after the normal greetings had passed.

'We'll take the stairs,' Travis said.

'It's your funeral,' Joey muttered even as he acknowledged the sheriff's wave with a nod.

Travis escorted Caroline to an out-of-the-way door marked *Private*. Someone, most likely one of Marlene's brothers, had added a skull sticker under the sign, along with one that read *Abandon hope all ye who enter here*. Someone had crossed out *hope* and written in *your lunch*.

'Be forewarned,' Travis said as he opened the door. 'Marlene has a weird sense of humour.'

As they descended a long, rather steep stairway, Caroline began to see what he meant. Marlene had decorated the walls with posters from horror movies, strange objects that looked like torture gadgets, and gruesome masks. The turn at the first landing brought into sight a full-sized blood-covered clown holding a wicked knife overhead.

She could not stifle a gasp.

'Yeah. Surprised me the first time, too. She put that there to keep her brother Jeremy out of her hair. He hates clowns.'

Like the normal fear of a bloody knife was not enough. If Caroline had not been with Travis, she might have turned tail and run at that point. As she approached the second landing, she took a deep breath to be prepared.

The vignette was disappointing at first. Nothing more than a simple wood and leather chair, in the Shaker style except for the inviting chintz pillow on the seat. Tatted doilies over the arms and on the back gave the scene a homey air, echoed by the family portraits on the wall. Then she saw a small box fastened to the leg of the chair. A blinking green light brought her attention to the attached cord that was plugged into the electrical outlet. Somehow subtlety seemed more threatening than the obvious had been.

Caroline sidled past, deciding right then and there that if she ever came back, she would definitely take the elevator.

'Stop right where you are,' Marlene said as soon as they entered her workroom/lab. She didn't bother looking up. 'I'm finishing up an autopsy. I suggest you wait upstairs and I'll join you in ten or fifteen minutes.'

Caroline spun on her heel, but paused and turned back when she sensed that Travis had continued into the room.

'I'm cool with you working while we chat,' he said.

'Did it occur to you that I might mind?' Marlene straightened up and flashed him a glare. 'I'm recording my work.'

'For posterity?'

'Ha, ha. No, I'll transcribe my observations later and use that to prepare the official report. And I'd rather not have to sort through a conversation for relevant information. Plus if the autopsy tape were ever reviewed in court, your comments would be . . . included.'

'Is that a not-so-subtle reminder to mind my manners?'

'If the cowboy boot fits . . . '

'Did you get a time of death?' he asked, nodding toward Jurgen Petersen.

Marlene ignored his question and instead called out a greeting to Caroline. 'You should make this big galoot take you someplace decent on your next date.'

'It's not a date,' both Caroline and Travis said, him a trifle too loud and her slightly too quick.

'Sounds like I hit a sensitive spot,' Marlene said with a gleeful chuckle.

'I'm here on business,' Travis said.

'I'm here to see Poor Fred.'

'Ongoing investigation,' he said.

'I feel sort of responsible for him,' Caroline said.

'And you just happened to arrive at the same time. Y'all ever hear of protesting too much? What now? Cat got your tongue? Fine with me. I'd rather talk than listen any day, which could be why I'm better at dealing with dead people than live ones.'

'Time of death?' Travis reminded her.

'Fine. I'll take a break from this. Let me

put Mr Petersen back in his designated drawer so he doesn't get overheated.' She wheeled the gurney to a wall of a dozen small refrigerators stacked three high and four wide.

'Which one is Poor Fred in?' Caroline asked. And where was all his stuff? The drawers didn't seem all that roomy.

Marlene closed the heavy door with a firm thud and adjusted several dials. 'These units were installed in the seventies and they're fabulous as far as temperature range. I can keep a Thanksgiving turkey frozen rock solid or warm up leftovers for lunch, but they're lousy at humidity control. The mummy needs near zero humidity and good air circulation to mimic the conditions he was found in.'

'So he's . . . ' Travis left the sentence open for her to fill in the blank.

'I'll show you in a minute,' she said, picking up her clipboard. 'First let me answer your earlier question. I still have a few more tests and I'll have a full report to you in the morning, but I know you never like to wait, so here's the scoop. As of right now, I'd call the time of death at two o'clock with a deviation possibility of four hours.'

'But that means he could have been killed while I was there,' Caroline said. 'That's impossible.'

'Why the spread? Can't you pin it down?'

'So far there are too many inconsistencies. For instance we know a body's internal temperature cools at the rate of one and a half degrees Fahrenheit per hour until it reaches the ambient temperature. Petersen's liver at six o'clock was eighty-three degrees, which translates to five hours dead.'

'So time of death is one o'clock,' Travis said.

'Except it's not an exact science. Other factors can throw that calculation off. If the body is naked or clothed, or if the deceased was thin or obese; even if the body is indoors or outdoors.'

'Or if there is a change in the ambient temperature,' Caroline said. The others turned to her. 'What? Oh, I was just thinking aloud. Sorry. Don't mind me.'

'No, no,' Marlene said. She came to stand in front of the other woman. 'That would be a factor. What made you think of it?'

'Well, the first time I went to the Petersens' they had the air-conditioner really cranked up high. Enid kept the doors to her conservatory closed, I assume because her plants like it warmer. When we went out on the patio to wait for the ambulance, I noticed how much cooler the air felt even though it was still quite warm outside. At first recall I reasoned that I must have been relieved to be away from the smell of death, but I think it might be more than that. Though when we passed through the living room on our way out, I don't remember it being warm in there.'

Marlene checked her notes. 'My temperature reading on site was seventy-one degrees. Not cold, but definitely cool.'

Travis joined the women at the foot of the stairs. 'If someone messed with the thermostat and significantly varied the temperature between the time of death and your exam, would that affect the validity of your conclusion?'

'Absolutely. The calculation assumes a constant ambient temperature. Without knowing what the variations were and how long each temperature was maintained, I can't be more accurate. On the flipside of that, I now understand why livor mortis and rigor mortis were at odds with the liver temp estimation.'

'What does that mean?' Caroline asked Travis from behind her hand.

'Rigor mortis is when the body stiffens — '

'Due to a chemical process in the muscles,' Marlene said. 'It starts within fifteen minutes of death and is usually apparent first in the smaller muscles like those found in the jaw and fingers. Rigor mortis is fully established in nine to fifteen hours and starts to wear off in twenty-four to thirty-six hours.'

'Again, not an exact measurement,' Travis said.

'Livor mortis is the purplish discoloration of the lower extremities that starts about two hours after death and is complete at approximately ten hours,' Marlene explained. 'Another indicator, but not a precise measurement.'

'Is there anything else that would pin down the time of death?' Caroline asked.

'I was just about to analyse the contents of his stomach, but I'm sure you don't want to hang around for that.'

'You got that,' Travis said. He gave Caroline's elbow a nudge towards the stairs.

'What about Poor Fred?' she asked, resisting his hint.

'Follow me,' Marlene said, bounding up the stairs two at a time. 'He's out in the stable.'

'Where?' Caroline called, pounding after her. 'Did you say you put him in the stable? I cannot believe you — '

'Take it easy,' Travis said, following close on her heels. 'Wait until you see the space before you put your spurs on.'

Marlene waited at the top of the stairs and hooked elbows with Caroline as she came through the door. 'We haven't kept horses since I was a kid. Grandpa insisted on having the horse-drawn hearse available for those clients who wanted it, even though it's over a hundred years old. His funeral was the last one to use it for that purpose. Now we only bring it out for special events and parades, and on those occasions we borrow horses.'

'Black, of course,' Travis said.

'If we can, but it's getting harder and harder to find horses broken to a carriage harness, much less a matched set of blacks.'

'So the old stable is now a storage shed?' Caroline asked.

Marlene threw open the door at the rear of the funeral home, revealing a wide concrete drive leading to the back of the lot. 'If you think a three-storey refurbished barn with a state-of-the-art air-quality-control system and security features that rival Fort Knox is a shed, then your answer is yes.'

Caroline blinked. Why would anyone put a security system on an old barn?

'All this is my brother Timothy's baby. He considered ditching the family business until he was offered an opportunity to be the regional distributor of Serene Caskets.' She entered a code into a keypad beside the huge door and it swung open smooth as glass. 'He stores his inventory in here, along with the antique hearse and both our limos.'

'I didn't realize an old hearse was worth so much,' Caroline said as they entered the temperature-controlled building. 'I mean, this space is amazing.'

'Yeah, but it's not for the hearse, or even the limos, though heaven knows we've spent enough on them. The security and air control are for the caskets.'

'Who would steal a casket?' Caroline asked.

'Just about every year somebody with half a brain comes up with the idea of stealing a metal casket to use as a cooler for their Halloween party,' Marlene said. 'Frat boys are the worst.'

'And now with the whole vampire craze, it's supposedly cool to have a coffin,' Travis said.

'I don't get it,' Marlene said. 'I grew up around them and no one ever thought I was cool.'

'You were just too cool too soon,' Caroline said.

Marlene snorted. 'Yeah, right. The problem is that none of these goonies think we have a security system because they have absolutely no idea what some of these pieces are worth. Not just the expensive woods you might have heard of like ebony, teak and mahogany. Rare African blackwood, Brazilian rosewood and Carpathian elm burl cost five to ten thousand dollars per pound. Even if the casket is veneered, it's still extremely valuable. We had a gold-plated casket that everyone wanted to look at, but it's gone now. The theft of even the less expensive models would still earn a charge of grand larceny.'

'Most of these kids are shocked to learn that a Class C felony carries a mandatory jail sentence of between one and ten years and a fine of up to ten thousand dollars, plus the guilty party can be required to pay restitution,' Travis said.

'I can't believe that,' Caroline said.

'Oh yeah. This is no slap-on-the-wrist crime.'

'No, I mean I can't believe someone actually bought a gold-plated casket. Talk about trying to take it with you.'

Marlene looked around as if to check for the eavesdropping presence of one of her brothers. 'I'm sworn to secrecy and can't reveal the identity of the buyer, but he's an easily recognizable name. He had us fit the casket with a comfortable mattress because he intended to take naps in it. We have learned that he's even slept through the night in it, supposedly to get used to the place where he'll sleep for eternity.'

'That is weird,' Caroline said. 'Creepy weird.'

'You know those Hollywood types better than we do,' Travis said.

'And over here is Fred's private suite.' Marlene entered a code into a security panel and pulled open a door. 'Each unit is separately controlled.'

Caroline stepped inside the ten-by-fifteen-foot room, the difference in temperature hitting her like a suffocating pillow. 'Wow, warm in here.'

'I've kept the temperature at a pleasant eighty-four degrees and the humidity at sixteen per cent. The system completely recycles and filters all the air in the space every two hours.'

On the left was a wall of shelves where all the items found with the mummy were laid out and tagged with numbers. To her right, Fred was seated on a gurney, propped up in a sitting position just like when he was found.

'The layer of cardboard on top of the pillow is so his back doesn't sink in,' Marlene explained. 'Air circulation is vital to maintaining his condition.'

'He actually looks quite comfortable,' Caroline said. Call it her imagination, but his face seemed more relaxed, as if he realized that someone was trying to establish his identity and determine the cause of his death.

Travis distracted Marlene just as he and

Caroline had planned so that she could slip the eagle statue in among Fred's belongings. She reached into her purse, but realized that since every item was tagged, anything new would stick out like a duck in a chicken yard and Marlene would become suspicious. She would have to come up with a different plan.

When she rejoined the others, Travis looked at her and raised an eyebrow. She gave her head a minute shake. He cocked his head to the side. She rolled her eyes up for a second and he nodded in response. Without words she'd understood his questions and answered them.

Did you do it?

No.

Why not?

Obvious if you think about it.

Right.

At the first break in Marlene's long description of some test she was running, Caroline said, 'I really have to be going. I appreciate your time and I'm glad to know Poor Fred is in such good hands.'

'We'll walk out with you,' Travis said. 'If you're ready to go too?' he asked Marlene.

'You two go on ahead. I've got a few things to check on and then I'll lock up.'

Caroline gave him a sideways glance. *Beat you to the door.*

No running.

Deal.

Ready, set, go.

They fast walked to the exit, reaching it at the same time, both breathless with stifled laughter.

'Outside, Caroline took a deep breath. 'Marlene is bound to think we're crazy.'

'Long as she doesn't spread any rumours about us dating, she can think whatever she wants.'

'Yes, that would be bad.' Caroline, suddenly serious, headed towards the parking lot and her escape vehicle.

Travis caught up to her and then shortened his stride to match her determined steps. 'Hey, don't get your panties in a twist. You don't want rumours any more than — '

'You're right about that.' She stopped and turned to face him, hands balled into fists and planted firmly on her hips. 'And for your information, my panties are none of your business.'

He held up his hand in defence. 'Just an expression.'

'Humpf.' She continued on towards her car.

'What are you going to do with the statue now? Because if you can't replace it, I'll — '

'I have a Plan B,' she lied.

13

Travis leaned back against Caroline's car, arms crossed over his chest, legs crossed at the ankles. 'You already have another plan? I thought that was Plan B that just failed?'

'Okay. Call it Plan C.'

'And that is?'

For lack of a better idea, she said, 'It's simple. I'll go back to the site, throw the statue into a crevice or bush or put it under a rock, then discover it all over again.' Not bad for last minute.

'Except what reason do you give the curious for being at the site?'

'Hiking?'

'By yourself? Not convincing.'

'Good point. You'll have to come with me,' she said.

'I don't hike.'

'Fine. I'll pack a picnic lunch.'

'Are you asking me out on a date?' he asked, faking surprise with exaggerated blinking.

'Hah! In your dreams.'

He pushed his cowboy hat to the back of his head with one finger and leaned towards her with an amused expression. 'Darlin', that's not even close to what I dream about.'

Caroline tossed her head, turned away, and climbed into her car. She stared at him with a stony expression until he moved away from her fender with a chuckle.

'Be ready at eleven thirty tomorrow,' he called after her. 'I'll pick you up.'

Caroline dithered about his comment all the way home. What did he mean? Was that supposed to mean he dreamed about her? She was so preoccupied with her thoughts, she almost walked up the stairs to her bedroom without answering Mimi's welcoming call.

'Is that you, Caroline?'

'Yes, ma'am.' She changed direction and headed into the kitchen.

'Good. I could use a hand. I'm in the middle of putting this coconut cake together and the potatoes au gratin is ready to come out of the oven.'

Caroline grabbed a couple of oven mitts and rescued the casserole before the topping toasted past golden brown. 'Do you want me to take out the ham, too?' she asked her grandmother.

'Sure. I just wanted to let the glaze melt.'

'Smells yummy.' She could appreciate the aroma even though she wasn't hungry.

'This isn't for us. We're taking these dishes

to Enid's when we make our condolence call tomorrow. Lou's coming with us. We should leave by twelve thirty.'

'Oh. Ah . . . well . . . '

'You're not trying to wriggle out of your proper — '

'No, ma'am. It's just that I made other plans for tomorrow.'

'Condolence calls are like funerals and births. Short notice is the norm. What's so important that you can't reschedule?'

She didn't want to tell her grandmother the real reason she wouldn't be around to take them to the Petersen ranch. If Caroline was going to take the fall for removing the statue, the fewer people who knew about it the better. 'Travis is picking me up at eleven thirty and we're going — '

'You're going on a date?'

If Mimi had had false teeth they would have fallen out of her mouth.

'It's not — '

'Hallelujah. I've been waiting for this day.'

'Don't let your little matchmaker heart go all a — flutter. It's not a date. We're going to the site where we found Poor Fred to see if we can discover anything that might help solve the mystery of his identity and murder. And I'm packing a lunch,' she finished in a rush.

'I see,' Mimi said. She'd finished putting coconut on the cake and placed the cover on the plastic plate, ready to deliver. 'Hmm. A non-date with food. What are you taking?'

'Huh?'

'For your picnic? What are you taking to eat?'

'Oh. I thought I'd make a couple of sandwiches and grab some chips and soda at the mini-mart on the way.'

Mimi's hand went to her throat. 'To think my own granddaughter would put together such a paltry picnic. Are you purposefully trying to shame me?'

'No one will even know what we eat but me and Travis, and he won't care.'

'What about the clerk in the store? What if someone else is picnicking at the same site? What if Travis's staff asks about his day off and he says you two went on a picnic? The obvious next question is what did you eat?'

Caroline threw her hands up in the air. 'Fine. I'll make a decent picnic.' She mentally ran through the fast-food possibilities and pre-made grocery store items. 'How does fried chicken, potato salad, coleslaw, and chocolate cake sound?'

'Excellent.' Mimi retrieved a large covered basket from the pantry. 'This is a perfect size for a picnic for two. Plenty of room for a variety of food.'

'Looks too big.'

'Nonsense. Remember you have to take plates, napkins and utensils.'

How much room did a few paper plates need? Caroline took the basket from Mimi and set it aside. 'I'll put it all together in the morning. Now, all this talk of food is making me hungry. What can I do to help with dinner?'

'Before we close the subject of tomorrow, we still need to talk about your condolence call. Lou and I can find another ride, but — '

'Do I have to go? It might get awkward if any of Enid's daughters ask me about finding the body and all that.'

'Your comfort is not the main concern.'

'Can you wait until two o'clock? I should be back by then.'

'Well . . . '

'And I would feel more comfortable walking in with you.'

'Very well. I'll call Lou and let her know we'll be going later than planned.'

'Thank you.' Caroline kissed her grand-mother's cheek. 'You're the best.'

★ ★ ★

Caroline slept late the next day after staying up half the night writing an article entitled 'The Language of Flowers, or What does Your Bouquet Say', for *Spring Bride* magazine. It would have been an easy fifteen-hundred-word article, except the new editor had pointed out her dislike of word repetitions, particularly within paragraphs. Caroline had struggled to comply, but really, how many synonyms were there for bouquet, bride and groom?

She took two headache tablets before heading downstairs. She had just enough time to get cake and potato salad from the grocery, drive through the chicken place, and return to pack up and be ready when Travis arrived. Taking a few minutes to get a cup of coffee to go was a necessary risk. She headed for the kitchen.

'Good morning, sleepyhead,' Mimi said. She sat at the table in the breakfast alcove with her half-empty cup, the coffeepot, and the newspaper open to the crossword puzzle. 'Is that what you're wearing on your date?'

Caroline looked down at her Princess Bride T-shirt and everyday jeans with the hole in the knee before remembering to say, 'It's not a date.' She grabbed a cup and poured herself some coffee.

'Regardless. Your outfit is appropriate for

doing yard work, not going out in public.'

Caroline sighed at the familiar argument. She'd grown up with Mimi's old-fashioned sensibilities and knew it would do no good to fight the inevitable. 'I'll change clothes in a minute.' And since that meant she would now have to ask Travis to stop at the store with her, at least she'd have a few minutes to relax and drink her coffee. She carried her cup to the table.

'Why don't you take that upstairs? I'll pack the picnic basket while you change. And you might consider putting on a dab of make-up,' Mimi said.

Caroline spun around and headed back up the stairs before she said something she might regret later.

Forty minutes later she returned, her hair blown into soft curls, daytime make-up in place, sleeveless white eyelet top, feminine but not fussy, over dark-wash denims and leather hiking boots appropriate for tramping around in the desert.

'You look very nice,' Mimi said.

'Thank you.' Caroline kissed her grand-mother on the cheek. She felt more confident knowing she looked good. And she especially appreciated Mimi's interference when she saw the admiring look on Travis's face when she answered his knock on the front door.

'Come on back to the kitchen to say hello to Mimi.'

No matter how casual the date, or not-date, her grandmother had always expected whoever picked up any of the girls to come inside and answer a few questions. Travis had been through the drill before and didn't seem to mind.

After the usual greetings, Mimi said, 'So where are you two kids going on your picnic?'

Caroline grimaced at being called a kid but Travis didn't blink. Even though Caroline had already told her grandmother, she held her peace so he could confirm their destination.

'We're going out to the campsite where Caroline found the mummy. If we retrace her steps, we might either find something we missed or jog her memory. Any little thing might help solve the mystery.'

Mimi frowned at his response.

'And it's a really nice day for a ride in the country.'

'You mean a drive in the country,' Caroline said.

'Nope. I've got my Harley running like a dream,' he said with a boyish grin. He rubbed his hands together. 'We'll be taking Ol' Sally out for her first spin in ten years.'

Mimi smiled at Travis's enthusiasm.

Caroline didn't share his fondness for the motorcycle. He'd been off on a road rally when she'd needed him most. And that had been the breaking point that had started her down the road to divorce. She'd finally forgiven him for not being there during her miscarriage, but she still distrusted his attachment to that infernal machine.

She was tempted to forget the whole non-date until she reminded herself of the real reason for the picnic charade. 'Let's go,' she said, grabbing the basket. 'We'll stop on the way . . . ' The unexpected weight stopped her in her tracks and nearly pulled her arm out of its socket. 'What the heck?' How much could paper plates and napkins weigh?

'Oh, I put in a few extras other than the fried chicken you asked for,' Mimi said.

'I didn't expect you to make our lunch,' Caroline said. 'I was going to buy — '

'Nonsense. You know how much I like to cook for you. Go, go. Enjoy.'

Travis picked up the basket one-handed as if it weighed mere ounces. 'You might have to sit on this,' he said with a chuckle as he followed Caroline out.

'Maybe I should drive myself. I could meet you there.'

'I'm just kidding. I'll strap it on with bungee cords.' He stepped in front of her and

251

turned to look her straight in the eyes. 'What's bothering you? You used to love to ride with me.' He shook his head. 'If you really want to drive . . . '

'It's just that it's been a long time since I've been on the back of a bike. I've outgrown — '

'You're never too old to feel the wind in your face.' Travis hooked his free arm through hers and propelled her down the steps and towards his motorcycle parked in the driveway. 'A little open-road therapy will make you feel like a kid again.'

'I'm not sure that's a good thing.' She eyed the bike with apprehension. The flame designs on the fenders looked as fresh and bright as when he'd had them painted in their senior year. Despite her protestations, a tiny ember of excitement warmed her insides. She'd almost forgotten the thrill of riding behind Travis, her arms wrapped tight around his waist.

'Hop on,' he said. When she hesitated he added, 'Mounting will be easier before I strap on the picnic basket.'

'Wait,' Mimi called from the porch. She carried a small cooler out to the driveway. 'You can't have a picnic without iced tea and cold fried chicken.'

'I could have come back for that,' Caroline said. 'Here, let me have it.' She took it from her grandmother and handed it to Travis.

Mimi followed her and motioned for Travis to come closer. When he leaned over, she said in a stage whisper, 'I tucked a little something special in there for you.'

'I heard that.' No telling what new matchmaking scheme her grandmother was up to. 'This better not be a ... a ... you-know-what,' Caroline said under her breath.

Mimi raised her hands in surrender. 'Just some Red Velvet cupcakes.'

Caroline squinted at her grandmother as if that would reveal any disingenuous plans she might be cooking up.

'Thank you,' Travis said with a confused expression. He turned back to his motorcycle and removed the extra helmet he'd strapped to the back of the seat. He held the new-looking black and silver headgear out to Caroline.

She hesitated.

He quirked his eyebrow at her. An unspoken question. His expression was a challenge, as clear as if he'd said *I dare you* out loud.

Resisting the urge to stick out her tongue at him, Caroline grabbed the helmet and climbed on to the motorcycle by swinging her right leg up and over, just like mounting a horse. Because the bike was resting on its kickstand, it leaned a little to the left. Yet another reason to feel off kilter.

She put on her helmet and waited for him to strap on the basket and the cooler.

Travis picked up his own helmet, similar in colour to hers, and put it on as he sized up the relatively small area left for him to sit. Leaning left, he raised his knee and kicked out to the side in a karate-like manoeuvre that ended with him astride the bike.

Caroline pushed against the backrest to give him as much room as possible. He took every inch, settling snugly between her thighs. His warmth generated an answering heat deep within her core.

He started the engine with a roar and slipped it into gear. The sharp turn-around in the drive caused Caroline to slip just a bit to one side, and she automatically wrapped her arms around his waist.

She watched the scenery as he guided the bike through town and accelerated on to the highway. She stretched to peek over his shoulder at the speedometer. The needle floated smoothly to sixty-five, the big machine purring deeply. Trusting Travis completely, she settled back to enjoy the ride. When he turned off the highway on to the dirt road, she was almost surprised they'd arrived at the mummy site so quickly.

He steered a zigzag path to avoid the worst of the ruts caused by too much traffic. As they got close to the site, signs directed their path. Someone had painted *Cars Only Parking Area* on a ragged piece of plywood and propped it against a mesquite bush. On the right a similar sign that identified the section reserved for RVs was lashed to a five-foot-tall sonora barrel cactus.

Travis drove right up to within twenty feet of the mouth of the cave before being stopped by a rope barricade.

'Howdy, folks,' called a man wearing an old-fashioned pith helmet, with a welcoming wave. He stood from his perch on a folding lounge chair shaded by the large green and white striped golf umbrella duct-taped to the back. Despite his precautions, his skin was darkly tanned, making his ice-blue eyes all the more startling.

He sauntered over with a self-important strut contradicted by his Ghostbusters T-shirt, wrinkled Madras-plaid Bermuda shorts, and earth-friendly sandals. 'Are you looking for the tent camping area? Just follow along this fence past that rise and you can't miss it.'

Travis switched off the engine and removed his helmet before dismounting. He held out a helping hand to Caroline. She swung one leg in front of her then slid off to a standing position. While she took off her helmet, Travis stepped over to their greeter.

'Hello,' he said, keeping his voice low and sociable. 'Name's Beaumont. Travis Beaumont. This is Caroline. What's going on?'

'Archie LaFont.' The man stuck his clipboard under his arm and shook Travis's hand. 'I'm your go-to guy for any questions about this place. I was one of the first to arrive on site.'

'So where is everyone?'

'Are you joking? Most treasure hunters are out at first light and don't come back till dusk.' He waved his arm to encompass the area from horizon to horizon.

Travis spotted signs of people spread out in the surrounding desert; a red hat here, a flash of an orange shirt, a glint of shiny metal.

'You're a Johnny-come-lately,' Archie said. He scratched the nape of his neck as he looked at his clipboard. Around a yellow star in the centre, most of the squares were marked with initials. 'I can give you a forty-by-forty-foot square beyond the parking lot that was only worked by a greenhorn. Could be something there. Or I could guide you to a prime spot. For a small fee, of course.'

'No thanks. We're just here to have a picnic lunch.'

'Oh.' Archie blinked, looking as if he just couldn't grasp the concept of someone turning down a chance to go treasure hunting.

'Why aren't you out there?' Travis asked. 'With the others?'

'Oh, I've already gone over my chosen squares with my Teknetics Omega 8000 metal detector. I've got a ten-inch coil on it and believe me, that baby can pick up a quarter buried a foot deep. Okay, nine inches, but no way did I miss any treasure. I always say if you don't find anything in the first few days, you're not going to.'

'And you're still here because?'

'My wife wanted her turn. She goes out. I watch the kids.' Archie glanced around. 'Oh, there they are.' He turned back to Travis. 'Everyone thinks the ropes are to keep people out, but really they're to keep the kids in.'

'That's horrible,' Caroline said, stepping forward.

'Just joking. Sheesh, lady, chill out. Omigod, it's you.'

Caroline backed up a pace.

'You're the woman who found the treasure.' Archie ducked through the ropes like an eager prizefighter. 'I have got to shake your hand. I never met anyone in person who actually found a life-changing treasure.'

'I didn't . . . I mean, it's not mine to keep or anything like that.' She looked to Travis while Archie reached out, grabbed her hand and pumped it up and down.

'It's an honour. A real honour. Boy, oh boy, Kissy is not going to believe this.' He shoved his clipboard at Travis with one hand, saying, 'Here, hold this for a sec.' At the same time he dug his cell phone out of his pocket. Then he scooted next to Caroline, leaned his cheek to within a fraction of an inch of hers, and said, 'Say cheese,' as he held up the phone to take a picture.

'You should ask permission before you do that,' Caroline said.

'Don't worry. The only person who'll see this is my wife, Kissy. Scout's honour. And she is going to freak out. Hey, know what would be cool? Let's take a few shots of you and me by the cave.'

'I'd rather not.'

'What am I thinking?' Archie slapped himself in the forehead. 'I should call her.' He dialled a few numbers as he talked. 'She's in the foothills today thanks to John Wayne. He's our eldest. She lets each of the kids pick a square for her.' The phone continued to ring. 'She's probably wearing the headset,' he explained apologetically.

'Perhaps we'll meet your wife some other time,' Travis said before turning to Caroline. 'Right now, I'm hungry.' He threw a significant glance towards the cave to remind her of their mission.

'Oh, yes. Me too.'

'You can use one of Mac's picnic tables.' Archie pointed to one of three food trucks.

'Won't that be rude?'

'What? No, not at all. Mac's out prospecting. Won't open for business until five thirty or six. Same as the others.'

Caroline didn't see any way to get closer to the cave. 'Well then the picnic table sounds like a good idea.'

While Travis unloaded the basket and cooler, and Archie begged his wife to pick up the phone, Caroline meandered across the open area trying to appear casual. The feeling of being watched was very strong, but she didn't see anyone. She stood at the very spot where she'd found Poor Fred. Should she just toss the eagle statue into the darkness in the depths of the cave?

'I wouldn't,' a gravelly male voice said.

She turned to face a young boy, aged ten or eleven. His white-blond hair stuck out in all directions, apparently a natural phenomenon rather than the result of products, and he was covered in brown dust. His worn T-shirt and carpenter shorts were wrinkled, and toes poked through his ragged sneakers. No one else was near. He stared at her with bright blue eyes.

'Did you say something?' she asked.

'You were thinking about prospecting inside the cave, weren't you?' he said, identifying himself as the unlikely owner of the deep voice. 'If there was anything left after the police cleared the area, it's already been picked clean by at least six others, including my father, and he's the best. I could guide you to a prime spot. For a small fee, of course.'

'No thanks,' she said. His last sentence sounded familiar. 'What's your name?'

'John Wayne LaFont.'

Of course. Why hadn't she recognized him? The boy was the spitting image of his father, especially his brilliant blue eyes. She had that strange feeling that you get when you know the word you want but it remains elusive, just beyond your reach. And why did that make her think of the *Titanic*, as if the tip of the iceberg wasn't the most important part? 'Shouldn't you be in school?' she asked him.

He squared his narrow shoulders. 'We're home-schooled. Ma got herself certified so we could treasure hunt year round as a family.'

Perhaps his mother should pay more

attention to grammar lessons and a little less to looking for gold. Not that it was Caroline's place to judge. 'That's nice,' she said, because it was the most non-committal thing she could think of.

She noticed Travis unpacking the basket and cooler. She headed in that direction and John Wayne kept pace at her side. 'We're going to have a picnic. Would you like to join us?' she asked.

'No thank you, ma'am. I already fixed peanut butter and jelly sandwiches for me and the kids.'

Although Caroline might appreciate his manners, she wasn't particularly thrilled to be called ma'am. As they approached the table, Travis snapped a red-checked tablecloth open and draped it over the weathered table in a single smooth motion.

'I didn't know you could do that,' she said with a grin.

'There's probably a lot you don't know about me.' He draped a white cloth napkin over his forearm, and bowed formally. Then he unpacked several plates from the basket, containing apples, oranges and bananas, an assortment of crackers. 'You've been away from home for more than ten years.'

'So have you.'

'Well, a man can learn a lot in that amount

of time: tactics, parlour tricks, skills.' He waggled his eyebrows on the last word.

'Behave yourself.'

She unpacked the cooler. A rectangular plastic container was stuffed with at least eight pieces of cold batter-fried chicken. A shallow dish held dill pickle spears, sweet gherkins, and both green and black olives. Removing another lid revealed assorted vegetables in bite-size pieces. There was potato salad. Coleslaw. 'Oh look, here's cheeses and deli meats to go with the crackers. That's what we were missing.'

Travis walked to the far end of the table to find room for the desserts: half a chocolate layer cake, half a lemon coconut, two strawberry custard tarts and a dozen large chocolate chip cookies.

Caroline put her hands on her hips and looked down the length of the table. 'I can't imagine what Mimi was thinking.'

'I hope you brought your appetite,' Travis said, shaking his head.

'I can do better than that.' She looked around and caught John Wayne staring at the table like Santa, the Easter Bunny and the Trick or Treat Fairy had just dropped by. 'Oh what shall we do?' she said in a loud, melodramatic voice. 'If only we had someone who could help us eat all this food.'

The boy was at her side in a heartbeat. 'Can I be of service?' he asked, not taking his gaze off the mountain of fried chicken.

'You mentioned *the kids* earlier. Do you have brothers and sisters?'

'Four.'

'Boys? Girls?'

'Two of each.'

Five kids. Okay, more than enough food for that many. 'Why don't you invite them to join us too?'

'If you don't mind, I'll just take a serving with me, and I'll share it with everyone. I'm in charge of the kids left in the camp while their parents are out treasure hunting, and it wouldn't be fair for some of us to eat in front of them.'

Caroline looked around but she still didn't see any children. 'How many more kids are we talking about?'

'Seven.'

'Is that total, or seven more?'

'Eleven altogether, twelve counting me.'

Travis gave a bark of laughter.

Caroline spared him a quelling look before saying to the boy, 'Okay. Bring them all.'

'Are you sure?'

'Absolutely. But we'll need more plates, silverware, napkins and — '

'I can handle that,' John Wayne promised.

263

14

John Wayne LaFont put two fingers in his mouth and let loose a loud whistle. Suddenly children appeared from all directions, from behind campers, beneath bushes, almost out of thin air, and lined up in front of the picnic table from tallest to smallest.

Even though they were all scruffy and dusty from playing outside, Caroline easily picked out the four other LaFont children, because they all had those distinctive blue eyes. She knew that somehow it was related to her discovery of Poor Fred, to Ernest the eagle statue that Julie had pilfered, and even to Jurgen Petersen's death. But for the life of her she didn't see any way that the LaFont family, or for that matter blue eyes in general, was connected to any of the other events.

She stifled the urge to tell Travis about her unexplainable hunch as John Wayne introduced each of the children in a rush of names: Cesar, Rita Hayworth, Cary Grant, Halina, Ciro, Paloma, Dougal, Kiara, Bernardo, and the five-year-old twins Ginger Rogers and Fred Astaire.

John Wayne quickly assigned tasks. Cesar

was sent for another tablecloth and eating utensils. Rita Hayworth was put in charge of washing the younger ones' hands and faces. Cary Grant and Ciro moved over another picnic table, by which time Cesar had returned with an assortment of paper and plastic dishes and utensils. Paloma and Kiara fetched juice boxes for the kids to drink. Paloma set the table and Bernado was sent to get the booster seats for the two youngest. Travis and John Wayne got two large umbrellas out of the back of the food truck and set them into the holes in the tables to provide a little shade.

'We never get to do anything,' Ginger Rogers grumbled as she slumped on to the bench.

Fred Astaire sat beside his sister and explained to Caroline, 'Our job is always *stay out of trouble.*'

'It's the hardest thing we do every day,' Ginger Rogers said with a dramatic sigh.

Within minutes the food was served, and with a nod of agreement from Travis, Caroline returned the unopened bottle of wine to the basket. They opted instead for the juice boxes Paloma and Kiara had so thoughtfully provided. Travis raised his in a silent toast to Caroline, and she responded with an identical motion.

To her relief there was enough of everything. Just barely.

She had a great time with the kids, but that meant she didn't have any opportunity to talk to Travis privately. And once they'd waved goodbye and started back down the road, the roar of the Harley engine made conversation difficult.

After parking in her driveway, he helped her carry the remnants of their picnic inside, and she offered him a glass of iced tea.

'Sure. Need some help cleaning up?'

'No, no.' She waved him to a seat at the table in the alcove and poured some tea for him. 'It'll just take a minute.'

He took the glass but remained standing, or rather leaning against the counter, boots crossed. 'I had the distinct impression earlier that you wanted to say something.'

She shrugged as she unloaded the plates from the basket directly into the dishwasher. 'No, I mean yes, I did then, but now it just seems silly.'

'How so?'

'I was thinking about Ernest . . . '

'Who?'

'The little eagle statue.'

'Oh, right.'

'I couldn't drop it in the cave like I'd planned to do. Not after John Wayne told me that area had been thoroughly searched by his father. I got a feeling that Archie LaFont was somehow connected to Poor Fred and to Jurgen Petersen's murder.' Her cheeks heated. 'Even as I say it I know it sounds embarrassingly ridiculous.' She gave a forced laugh. 'I guess I don't have your famous gut.'

'Gut feelings are merely information whose source we can't identify.'

'You're not saying you believe that Archie . . . '

'No. But gut feelings don't always make sense. Especially at first. You probably made the judgement that your feeling couldn't possibly be true and therefore stifled that line of thinking. Sometimes you have to be patient and trust your gut to reveal the rest of the information.'

Caroline tipped her head to the side as if listening. After a long moment she said, 'Nope. Zip, zilch, nada.'

He grinned. 'It's not like making a phone call, you know.'

'Good, you're home,' Mimi said as she entered the kitchen. She was dressed uncharacteristically in a small-brimmed straw hat, cotton shirtwaister with blue and purple flowers scattered across a white background, and simple huarache sandals. After she greeted Travis she turned to Caroline. 'You're not wearing that, are you?'

'I was just on my way upstairs to change.'

'You'd better hurry. Lou should be on her way over and we'd planned to leave in about ten minutes. Are you going out to the Petersens' with us?' she asked Travis as she started packing the food items she'd prepared earlier into two white cardboard boxes.

'No, ma'am. I have to work this afternoon.' He looked at his watch. 'May I load the car for you before I go?'

'Oh, that won't be necessary,' said Mimi. 'You go along to do what you need to do.'

'It's no problem. I have plenty of time. Let me carry that.'

Caroline left the two of them to go through the verbal minuet of politely accepting assistance. She was sure Travis would make the third offer required before a well-mannered person could accept help from a non-family member. A cultural ritual those raised above the Mason-Dixon Line never quite understood.

She took a record-breaking quick shower and dressed in a turquoise shell, tan safari jacket over matching slim skirt, and light brown strappy sandals, but by the time she hurried downstairs, Travis had left. Lou arrived dressed in a cotton shirtwaister with large pink and red roses. Her narrow pink belt matched her pink ballet flats and she'd strapped a pink straw bag to the front of her walker.

* * *

Caroline dropped Mimi and Lou off at the front door, and two strapping young boys carried in the food that the older women had brought. She had to park quite a distance away and was glad she'd worn comfortable shoes.

She knew the drill. First make sure that whatever food you'd brought got to the kitchen, where relatives, friends and/or church members logged the dishes into a journal and maintained the buffet table set up in the dining room. Then you sought out the bereaved family members to offer your condolences. This could take some time and could be a social landmine. As you worked your way through the crowd of fellow callers and other mourners, you had to socialize as you inched closer, keeping track of your turn and yet making room for certain callers like the minister or the mayor's wife to go ahead of you.

With that in mind, Caroline headed in edging around the crowd by following the wall. She caught a glimpse of Enid seated on what looked like a new couch, covered in pale pink brocade. Her sleeveless black dress with a jewel neckline and open cut-work jacket was flattering, even though it made her appear quite pale. Two of her daughters, also in black and one on each side, took turns addressing the callers of the moment, seated in two dark rose side chairs. The other two daughters worked the crowd, identifying anyone who should jump the line, introducing strangers to each other, and encouraging everyone to visit the buffet.

Caroline spied one of the girls headed in her direction, so she slid into the narrow space behind a large man in a grey suit. In doing so, she knocked over something on the bookshelf with her butt. He stepped forward, and she had enough room to pick up the framed photo, the sepia-toned wedding picture of Enid and Jurgen that she'd been shown on her first visit.

Suddenly reality shifted and she knew what her gut had been trying to tell her. Karl Volker was the spitting image of his grandfather; that was why he'd looked familiar when she'd met him. Jurgen Petersen was the man Karl had come all the way from Germany to find.

She had to show this picture to Travis. But how could she borrow it without explaining why to Enid? Glancing around, she tucked the frame inside her jacket and scooted towards the kitchen, not looking up until she recognized Mimi's shoes.

'What's wrong, child?'

'How long were you planning on staying?'

'Why on earth . . . '

'I found something,' she whispered. She tapped the back of the frame through her jacket. 'Travis needs to see this right away, but — '

'Then you need to leave. Don't worry about us. We can get a ride home no problem.'

'I feel terrible leaving you. I could come back.'

'Not necessary.'

'Are you sure?'

'Absolutely. Go. Go.'

Caroline gave her grandmother a kiss and ducked out the back door.

★ ★ ★

Travis entered the station and immediately had to fight the urge to turn around and walk out. When he'd requested a computer expert from state police headquarters he hadn't expected them to send Dolly Duprez.

'Afternoon, Sheriff,' Phyllis said. 'I have that report you requested and I'm prepared

271

to go over it in detail at this time.'

Although he appreciated the life-preserver his astute deputy had tossed his way, pretending to go over a non-existent report would only delay the inevitable. He might as well face Dolly and get it over with.

'Thank you, Phyllis. We'll get to that matter later.' He stuck his hand out. 'And Miss Duprez. Welcome back to Haven. I hope you had an uneventful drive down from Santa Fe.' She wore a standard uniform but she must have had it tailored to fit her overly voluptuous figure like a second skin.

'Hello, Travis. Is that any way to greet an old friend?' She stepped into his space and gave him a kiss on the cheek before he had a chance to back away. Her pungent perfume gave him an instant headache. 'You look surprised to see me.'

'I asked for someone who speaks German.'

'*Das bin ich.*' She flashed him a huge smile. 'That's me. Born Dolly Gretchen Ulrich. Duprez was my husband's name. I kept it after the divorce because it was easier.'

'Well then, the computer in question is over here.' He led her to the empty desk next to Bobby Lee's.

She sat down and pulled a CD out of her briefcase. 'Okay, let's see what this little baby has to tell us.'

'Don't you need the password?'

'Nope. My forensics program bypasses all that. What's this? Someone deleted all the files.'

'I guess we won't get anything . . . '

'Just an inconvenience,' she said. 'Most people don't realize that when they delete a file, the computer really only deletes its location out of the index. The data is still there until something else is written over it or until the storage device is formatted. I have a program that rebuilds the index based on the data.'

'Perhaps I should leave you to — '

'Not necessary. This will take a few minutes to run.' She sat back in the chair and crossed her arms. 'You promised to call me next time you were in the capital.'

'Ah, yes, well, I haven't been back to Santa Fe.'

'I see. Are you coming to the Law Enforcement Conference in March?'

'It's still a bit early for me to commit. I have to get through elections in November first.'

'I'm sure you won't have any problem getting elected. What have we here? Ah, seems like your suspect — '

'Victim.'

'Your victim had a fondness for neo-Nazi websites.'

'Not a big surprise considering he was a former German POW,' Travis said.

'Doesn't look like he was active. Just a lurker. I'll know more after I get this back to my lab.'

'Anything else?'

'Favourites links to a number of newspaper sites. He spent a lot of time searching the archives. Looks like he copied and saved a bunch of articles.'

'On what?'

'Old buildings being either torn down or renovated. Obituaries. Veterans' rights. Analysis of historical battles. Everything on that mummy found near here.'

'Can you give me a one-sentence summary on each of the articles? Maybe I'll see a pattern.'

'I can, but he saved dozens and dozens of articles, maybe a hundred.'

Travis laid a legal pad on the desk. 'Guess you'd better get busy. Do you need a pen?'

'Now just a minute. I do not — '

'I'll buy you dinner at the Arbor Inn if you're done by seven.'

'I'm on it.'

Phyllis turned back to the switchboard.

Travis retired to his office to read the reports the coroner had sent over. He'd waded through about ten pages when a

274

commotion in the other room caused him to look up.

Caroline marched directly into his office, closing the door behind her. He started to stand, but she waved him back into his chair. Then she unbuttoned her jacket. 'There's something I have to show you.'

'I like how this is starting.'

Caroline rolled her eyes. 'Please.' She held up the frame. 'May I have your attention on the photograph?'

'Okay. It's a nice old wedding picture. Where did you get it?'

'I borrowed it from the Petersen house without permission.'

'You mean you stole it? That's not something you should be telling the local sheriff.'

'I'll take it back. This is what my gut feeling about Archie LaFont was trying to tell me.'

'That you should get married?'

'Are you being obtuse just to aggravate me?' She held the frame up to within six inches of his face. 'Look closer.'

'Is that Enid and Jurgen Petersen?'

'Yes, and just like John Wayne is the spitting image of his father, Karl Volker bears a marked resemblance to this photo of a young Jurgen. I don't know why I didn't make the connection earlier.' She snapped her fingers. 'That's why Enid freaked when she met Karl.'

'When did that happen?'

'The day Jurgen died, Enid was at my office going over some plans for the vow renewal. Karl stopped by with some gifts for me to take to the hospital. She saw him and turned stark white.

'So Enid recognized the resemblance. Did she say anything to Karl?'

'Are you kidding? She ran out of there like the hounds of hell were on her heels.'

'Did Karl give any indication that he knew why she reacted to him that way?'

'He seemed just as confused as me.'

'If Karl did learn the truth, would he resent his grandfather's actions? After all, Jurgen left his wife and son to fend for themselves in post-war Germany while he changed his name and started a new life in America.'

'Maybe, but is that motive enough for murder?'

'I've had cases where folks were killed for less.' Travis's words were nearly drowned out by loud voices in the other room.

Caroline turned around to see what was going on.

Travis followed the noise and found Karl speaking harshly to Dolly.

'Settle down,' he said as he stepped

between the two. 'Dolly, may I introduce Karl Volker, a German citizen visiting our fair city.'

'For longer than intended,' Karl added.

'Karl, this is Officer Dolly Duprez of the state police. She's an expert in computer forensics.'

'Why is she looking at my grandmother's obituary?'

'This is Jurgen Petersen's computer. She restored what *he* was looking at.'

'I don't understand,' Karl said.

Caroline held out the wedding photo. 'This is Jurgen Petersen as a young man.'

Karl paled. 'He looks like my son Oswald, like a younger me.'

'We think Jurgen Petersen was probably the man you were looking for,' Travis said. 'DNA testing can verify that.'

Karl reached behind him and stumbled back until finding a chair and sitting. 'Mein Gott, I never . . . so tragic. Grossvater was alive and nearby all this time. And now I'll never have a chance to meet him.'

'Doesn't sound like motive for murder to me,' Caroline said out of the side of her mouth to Travis.

'Could be a guilty conscience talking,' Dolly said. 'Remorse can set in after the fact.'

Travis signalled Phyllis and she came over to stand behind Karl. 'You understand why

277

you'll be our guest until I clear up a few facts,' he said to the German.

Karl blinked up at him. 'I didn't kill him. Why would I do that? I wanted to talk to him, get to know him.'

'Maybe he didn't want to know you.' Dolly said. 'Maybe — '

'I'll handle any interrogations,' Travis said to her, his steely tone setting boundaries. He turned to Karl. 'If you'll follow Deputy O'Connor, we'll talk later.'

He picked up the framed photograph and handed it to Caroline. 'I think you need to return that, and since I have a few questions for Enid, I'll drive you.'

'Do you think I won't do it if you don't accompany me?'

'Not at all,' he said as he steered her towards the door.

'Hey,' Dolly called after them. 'What about that dinner you promised me?'

'Oh, right. Phyllis, call the Arbor Inn and tell them to put Ms Duprez's meal on my tab.'

Travis opened the door and didn't look back. But Caroline saw the daggers Dolly's glare threw at him. That brush-off was going to cost him.

15

In the car, Caroline called Mimi to learn that she and Lou were still at the Petersen ranch. She spent most of the drive listening while the older women took turns catching her up on the latest news. She'd missed seeing the mayor's wife, Mrs Keyes, dressed in a hideous green pantsuit, totally inappropriate. And her comments had precipitated a bit of a disagreement among the daughters. Mrs Keyes had said she supposed Enid would be selling the farm, since it would be too much work for her now that she was alone.

Two of Enid's daughters, Elsie and Suzanne, the youngest of the four, thought that was an excellent idea, but Bindie and Tilly said no way. Elsie and Suzanne wanted their mother to move into town so they could be closer and see her more often. Bindie and Tilly vehemently opposed the idea of selling the family legacy. The argument became quite heated until Pastor Dan stepped in. His advice to Enid was not to make any life-altering changes for at least a year.

When Travis and Caroline arrived at the farm, the crowd had diminished very little from her earlier visit. They lucked out and found a nearby parking spot.

'I'd prefer to talk to Enid in private,' Travis said as they walked to the door. 'Can you bring her outside to the patio?'

'Last time I was there, it was packed with people.'

'I'll take care of that.'

'How? If you ask people to leave, they'll want to know why.'

'Ah, I'm a uniformed lawman and I have a mean you-look-guilty-of-something stare. Don't you worry. I can clear a room in ten minutes. You concentrate on bringing Enid out alone.'

'After I replace the photo.'

'No, I'll hang on to that for now.'

She gave him the frame and a puzzled expression. 'I don't understand where you're going with this.'

He put an arm around her shoulders and gave her a squeeze as he kissed her on the temple. 'I'm trusting my gut to lead me to the rest of the information. Just like you did.'

Should she tell him it wasn't her gut? Her butt was responsible for knocking over the picture frame that had led to the revelation. Maybe not.

They separated inside the front door. Travis made a beeline for the patio, and Caroline worked her way smiling and nodding closer and closer to the couch where Enid held court.

'Pardon me,' she said, stepping past a petulant teen intent on texting, a middle-aged woman with a stunning hat, and a thin older woman who had bright-orange hair, bright red lipstick, and a huffy attitude that Caroline ignored.

She approached the couch. 'My condolences.'

Enid stood and gave her a hug. 'Thank you. Mimi said you came but I didn't see you.' She introduced Elsie and Suzanne. 'Bindie and Tilly are around somewhere.' She waved her handkerchief in a helpless motion. 'I'm a bit overwhelmed by all these people.'

'You should probably take a break,' Caroline suggested.

'Oh, I don't know.'

'Your daughters can handle everything for a short while.'

'Maybe later.'

'Now would be the perfect time.' Caroline leaned forward and whispered, 'Travis would like to ask you a few more questions. In private.'

'He's here?'

'On the patio.'

Enid gave a deep sigh before excusing herself for a few minutes.

'I'll go with you,' Elsie said.

'Me too,' Suzanne said. 'You shouldn't be alone at a time like this.'

'I really need you girls to stay here and talk to our guests. Just for a few minutes. Caroline will walk with me and she can be depended on to call you if I need anything.'

'I promise,' Caroline said to the *girls*, who were old enough to be her mother. She took Enid's arm and led her away. The older woman seemed more delicate, more fragile than she had only a few days before.

True to his word, Travis had cleared the patio of people.

Enid gave a sigh. 'Ah, silence. It's true. You don't appreciate the simple pleasures until they're gone.'

Travis held a chair for Enid and nodded to Caroline to take the third seat at the small table he'd moved to the far end of the enclosed patio. 'How are you holding up?' he asked Enid.

'As well as can be expected. I appreciate you coming. Caroline said you had more questions.'

'Just a few minor items to clarify. Let me first tell you that the coroner's report confirms that your husband did not die of natural causes. This is now officially a murder investigation.'

Enid nodded. 'I was afraid that would happen after hearing Marlene's comments, but I thought she said it could take up to six weeks to get the results back from some of her tests.'

'That's true. But Lou always said scientific tests were to convince the jury of what cops found in their investigation.' He put a small tape recorder on the table and turned it on. 'We have a suspect in custody. Karl Volker.'

'But he never even met Jurgen. Why would he . . . '

Travis slid the wedding photo to a spot in front of Enid. 'Tell me what happened,' he urged in a soft voice.

She didn't pick up the frame. In fact she seemed to avoid looking at it. 'I guess it started that morning when I met Karl Volker. I knew immediately he was related to my husband. The resemblance was uncanny. At first I thought he was Jurgen's son, and when I returned home I accused him of infidelity.

'Of course, he denied any such possibility, but he was intrigued that I'd seen a man in his image. We went into his office and called up a file on his computer. He asked me if the man I'd met was the man in the picture. I said he was, but it was the article that caught my attention.'

'The article he'd called up on the

computer?' Travis clarified.

'Yes. It was an obituary of Karl's grandmother. I asked Jurgen if he'd been married to her, and he said yes. I was horrified, flabbergasted. He said that at least she'd given him a son. Suddenly it was clear that Jurgen was not the man I thought he was. That was not even his real name.' She looked over at Caroline. 'How could I have lived with a man for more than sixty years and not know his real name?'

'I'm sure that was quite a shock,' she said.

'What did you do?' Travis asked.

'I cried. I ranted. But nothing ruffled his calm. He told me to get used to the idea, because he'd named Karl Volker as his heir. He intended my family's farm to go to his grandson by another woman.'

'That's cold,' Caroline said.

'It was like a splash of icy water on my emotions. Suddenly I realized that Jurgen had no feeling for me, had never had any. He was only after the land. And I also realized that he didn't want a vow renewal ceremony; he wanted a wedding. Since his German wife had still been alive until recently, our marriage wasn't legal, and that meant he wasn't entitled to any of my inheritance.'

'Common law . . .'

'Not applicable,' Travis said. 'I'd have to

284

check to be sure, but I don't think that clock started ticking until his wife died.'

'So I told him I'd changed my mind and I wasn't going to marry him. He threatened to reveal that my children were bastards.'

'And that made you angry?'

'Made me sad. They're his daughters, too.'

'So you agreed to marry him?'

'No. I refused to hand over my farm to him just so he could leave it to his grandson. He became sarcastic when I called it my farm, claiming that without him I'd still be wearing flour-sack dresses and shoes only on Sunday. Without his intervention, my father would have married me off to Ol' Jeb Reynolds, sold the farm, and moved to California to open a soda shop.'

'What did he mean by *his intervention?*' Travis asked.

'Exactly my question,' Enid said.

'And his answer was . . . '

'That it was his lunchtime and we would have to continue our discussion later.'

'What did you do?' Caroline asked.

Enid shrugged. 'I fixed his lunch.'

Caroline sat back in her chair, dumbfounded. 'After all that, you just went into the kitchen — '

'Let her finish,' Travis said, not unkindly, but as if he expected something important.

Enid stared down at her hands and twisted her handkerchief into a damp cloth pretzel. 'That nice young man Karl Volker had nothing to do with Jurgen's death. I don't want to face my maker with his fate on my conscience.'

'You don't have to.'

Enid raised her chin. 'I put some tincture of *Passiflora incarnate* in Jurgen's elderberry wine. Passionflower's constituents include harmine, which was originally known as telepathine because of its peculiar ability to induce a contemplative state and mild euphoria. It was used by the Germans in World War II as truth serum.

'When Jurgen lay down on the couch for his siesta, I questioned him about my father. At first he wouldn't answer me. He wanted to talk about Walther, the prisoner who worked for us on the farm. Jurgen revealed that it wasn't me his so-called friend was afraid of; Walther was afraid of Jurgen, and rightfully so. Jurgen killed Walther when his discovery of gold empowered the subservient man to stand up to the bully. He was worried that the mummy would be identified and that the trail would eventually lead to him. The pistol he used to shoot Walther is in his wall safe.'

'Do you know Walther's last name?'

Enid shook her head. 'I'm not even sure

that was his real name. I once asked him about the scar on his left temple and he said he'd suffered a head wound in Africa. A sweet, sweet man who would never have hurt a fly, but I'm not sure he was all there, if you know what I mean. Sometimes he referred to himself as I wein, and he'd forget my name and call me Laudine.'

Caroline turned to Travis. 'He meant her to have it.'

'How will you explain — '

'I won't have to. It belonged to her all along.'

'What are you talking about?'

Caroline took the little eagle statue out of her purse and gave it to Enid.

The older woman turned it over and over in her hands, tears in her eyes. She traced the engraving on the bottom with her finger. 'What does it say? I don't have my glasses.'

'It says, 'For Laudine from Iwein, trapped in the land of his foes 1945 E.W'.' Caroline recited from memory.

'He carved it while working here. I think he tried once or twice to warn me about Jurgen. My life would have been so different if I hadn't been blinded by Jurgen's charming façade. I should have known better. I should have listened to my father, who was dead set against me marrying a former POW.'

'Is that why Jurgen killed him?'

'How did you know that?'

'I researched the official reports of the so-called hunting accident. I always doubt cases where the only witness is also the main beneficiary.'

'Under the influence of the telepathine, Jurgen admitted, no, bragged about killing my father.' Tears slid down Enid's cheeks and she balled her hands into tight fists. 'He was so proud of his brilliant plan. First kill my father, then marry me, then kill me off too, and he would own the farm free and clear.'

'But he didn't kill you.'

'I did point that fact out. For a fraction of a second I held out hopes that he'd fallen in love with me, or that he cared about our daughters.'

'No, huh?'

'It took the returning POWs nearly two years to reach home. Jurgen learned from a friend that his wife had survived the war. Since that made our marriage invalid, he had to wait for her to die, and then marry me all over again. At least that kept him mostly civil all these years, although he never expected her to live so long.'

'I'm surprised he didn't go to Germany and kill her off himself,' Caroline said.

'Oh, he thought about it. Problem was, he

was afraid to apply for a passport. Don't forget, he was living under an alias.'

'He could have obtained a fake passport or paid an assassin,' Travis pointed out.

'Oh, he thought of that, too. The key word there is *paid*. Jurgen was so thrifty, his wallet creaked when it was opened. That's why I knew something was really wrong when he let me plan a big ceremony for the vow renewal. Oh, he laughed about that. Me in a white wedding dress. At my age. The girls as bridesmaids. Said we had no idea how ridiculous we were going to look.'

When Enid hesitated, Travis said, 'And that's when you put the pillow over his face.'

'I just wanted him to stop talking.' Enid rocked back and forth, tears flowing unchecked. 'I couldn't bear to hear any more. He laughed at my naiveté. He said I was still fat and stupid and gullible. I just wanted him to go to sleep so I didn't have to listen to his laughter. Why didn't he just go to sleep?'

'And then he was quiet.'

'Such an evil man.' Enid sniffed and wiped her eyes. 'I left him and went to the garden to pray.'

'You understand that I have to arrest you,' Travis said. 'After we see the judge you can post bond, but you will have to stand trial.'

Enid nodded. She gave him a half-smile and shrugged. 'What are they going to do to me? The death penalty? Life in prison? I'm eighty-eight years old. I'll probably die before I exhaust all my appeals.'

'But it was an accident,' Caroline said. 'You didn't mean to kill him.'

'I'm afraid in my heart I did.'

'But he admitted he planned to kill you. That makes it self-defence. I can't believe a jury would convict you of murder.'

'I'm much more worried about meeting my Saviour. I always thought of myself as a good Christian woman, but in the last few days I learned I've been living in sin most of my life.' Enid blinked rapidly and sniffed.

Voices drifted in from the kitchen.

'And I'm worried about telling the girls.' She dabbed at her eyes with a soggy handkerchief. 'I guess I should do that right away. Before you march me out of here in handcuffs.'

'That won't be necessary,' Caroline promised. 'I'll fetch your daughters, and then I'll get Lou and Mimi to help send all the callers home.'

'Will you help me write a statement for the newspaper? I'd rather not leave it to the gossips.'

'Of course I will,' Caroline said, her throat

tight. She patted Enid's hand and left on her errand.

★ ★ ★

Fifteen minutes later Caroline and Travis stood outside the front door watching the cars drive away. Inside, Lou and Mimi helped Bev clean up while giving Enid and her daughters some privacy on the patio.

Travis pulled his handcuffs out of his belt loop. 'I guess I can't wait any longer.'

'You're not going to use those on her?' Caroline was horrified.

'Trust me. They are absolutely necessary.'

'But . . . but . . . ' she sputtered, unable to comprehend, much less respond. And then their conversation was interrupted.

A news van from the El Paso TV station pulled up and Arlene Couch, investigative reporter, stepped out. 'Sheriff Beaumont,' she called with a little wave, and came towards them, her stilettos clicking like a time bomb. 'I got your call. What's the big scoop that's going to get me national airtime?'

'You called her?' Caroline muttered between clenched teeth. She couldn't believe her own ears.

'Trust me,' Travis whispered in an aside before he flashed Arlene a smile. 'You're just in time. Keep your eyes open and you'll see for yourself any second now.'

'Give me five minutes to get my cameraman in place,' she said, beckoning frantically to the guy in the van with one hand while she dug a lipstick out of her purse with the other.

Travis turned, but before he could re-enter the farmhouse, Caroline grabbed his arm. 'How could you do this to a sweet little old lady like Enid?'

'It's my job. Did you forget Enid murdered her husband?'

'Yeah? Well, justice can be a bitch. Jurgen deserved to die.'

'This isn't the Wild West any more, and we don't settle scores by taking the law into our own hands.'

'But you can't — '

'I have to.' Travis shook off her hand and entered the farmhouse with a determined set to his jaw.

Caroline followed. She watched Travis handcuff Enid and lead her out into the glare of the camera's lights. He put her in the squad car and gave a few terse answers to the reporter's eager questions. As he drove away, the cameraman ran to stow his equipment and then the news van careened down the drive after the squad car.

Enid's daughters came out on to the front

porch. The girls stood arm in arm. Caroline was glad they were supporting their mother.

'Momma made us promise we wouldn't go to the jail,' Suzanne said.

Lou, pushing her walker, stepped out behind them. 'If you girls want to pack a small bag of toiletries for your mother, we'll drop them off on the way home.'

Elsie and Bindie left to do as suggested. The other two daughters soon followed. Lou patted Caroline's arm before she too went back inside.

Caroline lingered, turning the last hour over in her mind. She just couldn't understand what had gotten into Travis. She'd never seen him so hard-nosed and uncompromising. Had his career changed him that much?

16

'Nice party.'

Caroline didn't have to turn around to know that Travis was standing behind her. 'Thank you.' She'd done a good job of avoiding him recently. She still hadn't forgiven him his treatment of Enid.

'It's the first get-out-of-jail-free party I've ever been invited to.'

'First one I've ever planned.'

'I haven't thanked you for your help on the investigation.'

'No problem.' She spared him a brief glance. They stood in silence for several minutes.

Enid spied them and came over to give Travis a big welcome hug. She looked years younger, ten pounds thinner, and couldn't seem to stop smiling.

'Congratulations,' Travis said. 'That was the fastest acquittal I've ever seen.'

'Not that I'm complaining, but the state prosecutor really blew it by being greedy. Exactly as you said he would.'

'What do you mean?' Caroline asked.

'Didn't Travis tell you?' Enid slapped his shoulder. 'Caroline probably thinks you were being a jerk when you arrested me.'

'That's not far from the truth,' Caroline admitted.

'Is that what's been eating your craw? Didn't I tell you to trust me?'

'I don't understand.'

'When we had a few minutes alone, Travis told me that such a high-profile case with international interest would cause the state prosecutor to practically salivate, he was so eager to make a name for himself. My best chance was for him to get overconfident.'

'So that's why you called the reporter,' Caroline said to Travis.

He nodded. 'And it worked. The state prosecutor went for premeditated murder, while every woman on the jury was thinking justifiable homicide. Even the three men would never have convicted a sweet little old lady on murder one.'

'You would have been acquitted even if he'd lowered his sights and the charges,' Caroline said, giving Enid a kiss on her cheek. 'Seems I owe you an apology,' she said to Travis.

'For what?'

'All the terrible things I've been thinking about you.'

'Terrible? Really?'

'I should have trusted you.'

'I'll try to think of a way for you to make it up to me.'

Enid turned to Travis. 'By the way, Karl has been looking for you. Wants to introduce you to his boys.'

'Oh, I'm glad they made it. I'm sure I'll run into him soon.'

'Do you hear that?' Enid's eyes lit up. ''String of Pearls'. My favourite song. If you'll excuse me, I'm going to find a handsome young man to dance with.'

'What am I?' Travis asked, throwing his arms wide. 'Chopped liver?'

'You know who you should ask to dance,' Enid called back over her shoulder.

Travis looked down at Caroline with a slow smile. Tousled red-gold curls, laughter in her brown eyes, summer freckles across her nose. Her lips in that delicious pout that begged for a kiss.

'We haven't danced together in a long time,' she said.

'Maybe we should try doing something else together that we haven't done in a while.'

She raised her eyebrows.

'Like going on a date. Say dinner and a

movie in El Paso next Saturday night?'

'A real date? That's a big step. Are you sure we're ready?'

'We can discuss it during a dance,' he said, holding out his hand. 'Or three.'

She smiled and took his hand.

Five interesting things about Laurie Brown:

1. I am a true shoe-a-holic and have over a hundred pairs of shoes to prove it. (This addiction probably stems from having to wear ugly brown orthopaedic oxfords as a child.) Now I've reached a point where if I buy another pair, one of the others has to go. Either that or my office/overflow closet will become just a closet and then where will I write?

2. Cotton balls make me shiver like when fingernails scratch across a chalkboard. I can't bear to touch them. I swear they make noise when they're squeezed, but no one else in my family seems to hear it.

3. Cooking shows on television fascinate me but they haven't made me any better at coping with kitchen duty. Thankfully my husband is marvellous. Don't you just love a man who cooks?

4. I love crossword puzzles but must restrict myself to the one in the Sunday newspaper.

If I buy those little books of puzzles all I wind up doing is copying the answers found in the back.

5. I can drink coffee anytime, anywhere, any flavour. Love it.

We do hope that you have enjoyed reading this large print book.

Did you know that all of our titles are available for purchase?

We publish a wide range of high quality large print books including:
Romances, Mysteries, Classics
General Fiction
Non Fiction and Westerns

Special interest titles available in large print are:
The Little Oxford Dictionary
Music Book
Song Book
Hymn Book
Service Book

Also available from us courtesy of Oxford University Press:
Young Readers' Dictionary
(large print edition)
Young Readers' Thesaurus
(large print edition)

For further information or a free brochure, please contact us at:
Ulverscroft Large Print Books Ltd.,
The Green, Bradgate Road, Anstey,
Leicester, LE7 7FU, England.
Tel: (00 44) 0116 236 4325
Fax: (00 44) 0116 234 0205

THE DEATH OF BRIDEZILLA

Laurie Brown

When Caroline Tucker's wedding-planning business goes bust, she gets sucked into organising her cousin Barbara's nuptials, in Haven, New Mexico. But Barbara turns out to be a Queen Bride — a Frankenbride — Bridezilla even — and driving Caroline round the bend. And when Barbara's car crashes, Caroline is accused of her murder! Luckily, the arrestingly handsome Sheriff, Travis Beaumont, is on the case — not so luckily, he's also Caroline's ex-husband. She's not impressed with this unwanted blast from the past, but she will have to work closely with him if she wants to avoid a future behind bars.

ALWAYS THE BRIDE

Jessica Fox

Nobody gets it right all the time. But Zoe Forster always strives for perfection. So when the fortune-teller at her hen party predicts she will marry twice, she's seriously unimpressed. Everyone knows Zoe and Steve are meant to be together. Still, even a marriage made in heaven has to survive in the real world and, a year in, things are getting predictable. Then super-sexy movie star Luke Scottman makes a repeat appearance in Zoe's life, and Zoe and Steve make some unwelcome discoveries about each other's less-than-perfect pasts. It seem the fortune-teller's prediction is about to come true after all . . .